GAGE

GAGE

A SENTIENT RULER ROMANCE

IMOGEN KNOWED

Copyright © 2026 Mouse Potato Games, LLC
All rights reserved.

No part of this publication may be reproduced, distributed, or transmitted in any form or by any means, including photocopying, recording, or other electronic or mechanical methods, without the prior written permission of the publisher, except as permitted by U.S. copyright law.

The story, all names, characters, and incidents portrayed in this production are fictitious. No identification with actual persons (living or deceased), places, buildings, and products is intended or should be inferred.

NO AI TRAINING: Without in any way limiting the author's and publisher's exclusive rights under copyright, any use of this publication to "train" generative artificial intelligence (AI) technologies to generate text is expressly prohibited. The author reserves all rights to license uses of this work for generative AI training and development of machine learning language models.

Paperback ISBN: 979-8-9874825-7-5
Ebook ISBN: 978-1-972670-27-9

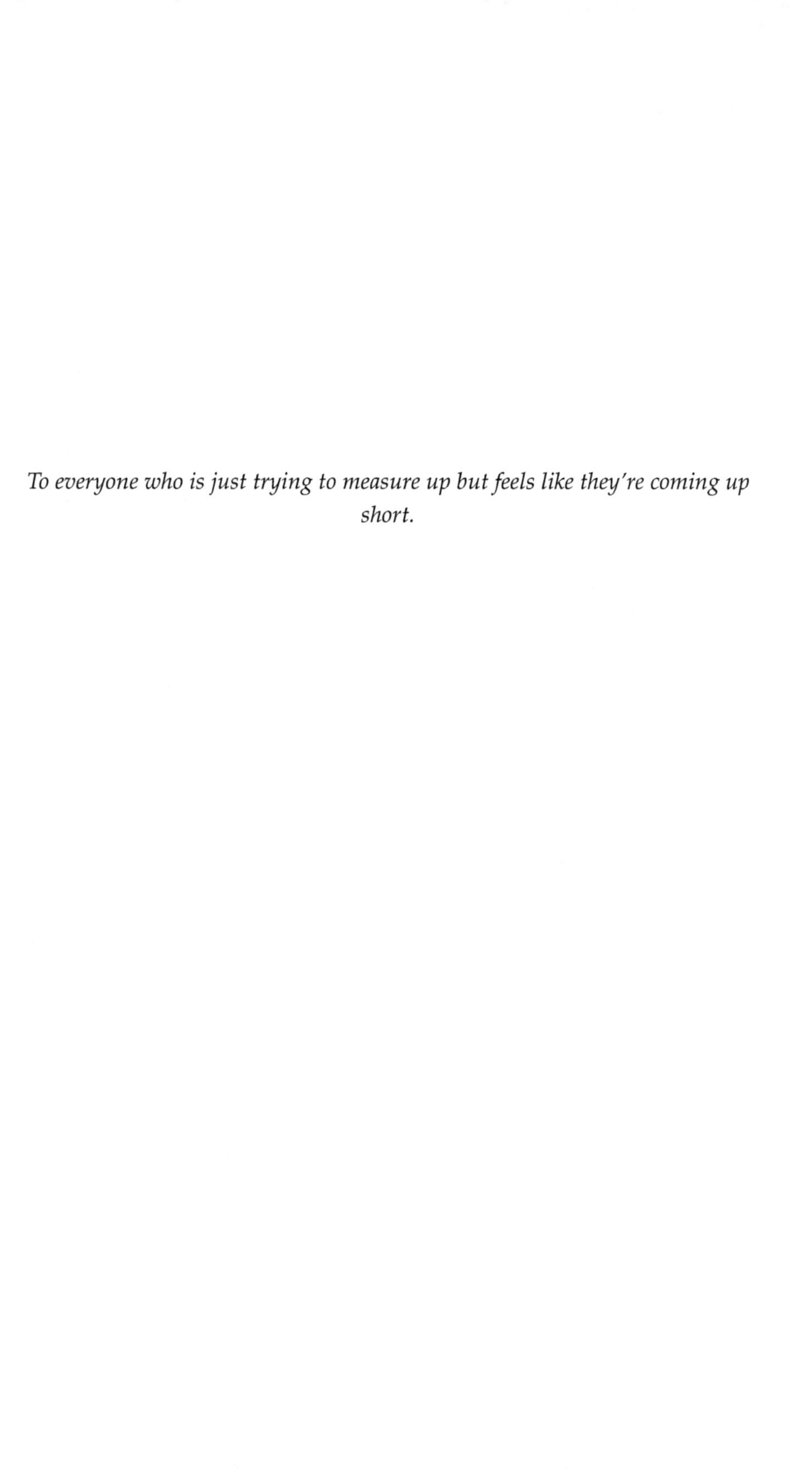

To everyone who is just trying to measure up but feels like they're coming up short.

CONTENT WARNINGS

This book has explicit descriptions of sexual acts.

While all sex is consensual, some acts may be considered dubious or coerced.

CHAPTER 1
ALICE

My phone buzzes. The screen shows "MOM," all caps, her photo an ancient selfie from her Tae Bo phase.

"Hi, Mom," I say, an annoyed groan already locked and loaded.

"Alice! Baby! Big day tomorrow!" Her southern accent twangs in my ear.

I unleash the prepared groan. "Mom, twenty-seven is probably the most boring of all birthdays."

"Well, tomorrow is special, honey. That's why I called." She drops her voice to a weird, earnest octave.

Please don't tell me you're coming to visit.

I hold my breath.

"Anyway, listen," she says, and I can tell she's getting her Serious Mom voice ready. I'm hoping it's not a lecture about how I need to find a man or start using retinol, because both are true, and I don't want to hear it. "So, you know the legend of our family, right?"

"Sure," I say, dry and annoyed. It's a story I've heard tons of times and one I've never believed. "We're descendants of some ancient king who turned everything to gold, but somehow none of us benefited from any sort of generational wealth."

"Yeah, well, it's a true story."

I snort. "Sure, and you're secretly a My Little Pony."

"No, but your uncle Chance is."

"Huh?"

There's silence on the line, which is more menacing than yelling. I check to see if she's muted herself, because she does that occasionally —always a welcome reprieve from her normal onslaught of over-momming.

She hasn't.

I hold my breath yet again, ready for the bad news that always follows this type of non-accidental-muting silence. I imagine she's squeezing the bridge of her nose right now, acting as if this will hurt her more than it will hurt me—which it never does.

The queen of terrible timing finally says, "Our family, on the women's side, has a…hereditary condition. A gift. Some say a curse. Kind of like King Midas. It activates on our twenty-seventh birthday."

I sit down on the nearest cleanish surface. "Mom, are you day-drinking?"

"Don't be a smartass, Alice, this is important." Her tone cuts through me, making me sit tall like I'm five years old and eager to please her—which is half true. "I need you to listen and be prepared."

"Prepared for what, exactly? Am I about to start turning everything I touch into gold?" I laugh at the ridiculousness of it all.

"Not gold," she says. Her voice is glassy—thin, sharp. "Please, you have to listen. Starting at midnight, anything you—put inside yourself —will turn into a person."

She says "inside yourself," with a breathless rush. For a second, I think she means, like, eating or maybe spiritual enlightenment or whatever, but she clarifies quickly: "If you put something in your vagina, it becomes a human. A fully grown one. And they'll be obsessed with you."

I blink, waiting for the punchline, waiting for her to say, "sike" in a way that would be wholly uncharacteristic of her.

She doesn't.

"Okay, wow, that's a new one, Mom."

"I'm serious." She's whisper-yelling now. "It happened to me, and to your grandmother, and her mother before her. All your aunts. All your cousins."

I consider hanging up—not entertaining whatever the fuck this is any further—but I am riveted, desperate to know what the end goal of all of this is. "Mom, this isn't even a funny joke."

"I'm not joking! This is why I always told you not to use tampons."

"You told me not to use them because Aunt Janice got toxic shock wearing a tampon too long on an international flight."

"Well, that's sorta true. She didn't factor in the time zone change when she flew to Japan for her twenty-seventh birthday. She got stuck with a naked man in a tiny plane toilet." She sighs. "She had that douche…well, tampon following her around for years before she finally flushed him out of her life."

I open my mouth and then close it. I want to say something clever or snarky, but I can't. "Mom, I…I don't understand what you're trying to do right now, but please let me in on the joke."

"I'm trying to warn you: don't put anything in there you wouldn't want to live with forever. They come out obsessed with you and…with the exact personalities you'd think they have, but still they manage to surprise you…it's hard to explain."

I quip, "Okay, so like, don't stick any wet noodles inside me. Sure, I get it."

"I'm being serious! You joke now, but after midnight tonight, anything you put inside there will become a person. A real person, Alice! You have to be careful. It's permanent." She sighs and says something I've never heard her say before. "Alice, I'm sorry. I should have prepared a speech or something. I'm fucking this up…"

The sincerity, paired with the uncharacteristic apology, makes me deeply uncomfortable for reasons I couldn't explain even if I tried. I open my fridge for comfort, stare at the bleak options. Comfort, unfortunately, does not come in the form of expired condiments or takeout I should have thrown out weeks ago. I close the fridge and sit back down.

"Mom, this is…it's just unbelievable."

Her voice changes again, obviously adjusting her manipulation tactics. "Alice, your father…he was…well, it's how I got him."

I scoff, "Yeah, sure," picturing my father. Even at middle age, he has perfect hair and a large, square-shouldered physique that would make the most dedicated gym rat jealous. His good looks contrast with his personality: the world's most boring accountant.

"He was my…" she pauses and says through a cough, "calculator watch."

I stand again because sitting feels too passive for whatever this is. "You're telling me my father used to be a calculator watch? So what? That's why he's really good at math and dresses like it's still the eighties? Is that also why he has the social capacity of a coin cell battery?"

"Alice," she hisses. "Don't speak about your father like that. He is a good man. He adapted, and it's not his fault he's boring. But yes. That is why. Like I said, they have the personality you would expect."

I consider my father further, and the more I think about him, the more it makes sense…he is decidedly calculator-watch-like.

She adds, "That's why I'm warning you: don't pick anything you wouldn't want to live with." She says it as if my shoving something up there eventually is a foregone conclusion.

"Mom, why the heck would you shove a calculator watch up there to begin with?"

"I had made some mistakes—chosen unwisely. I thought he'd be good for me—he got me through some tough math classes. And I was right! He became an amazing man!"

I'm pacing now, hoping that movement will guide me through this conversation. "Even if this is real, why would you wait until the literal night before to tell me?"

She sighs, long and sad. "I wanted you to have a normal life. Didn't want you to develop a complex. Everyone takes the news differently, but most who learn early spend their whole life worrying about it. I just…wanted you to not worry about all this."

"So what, I'm supposed to just abstain from—" I gesture vaguely at my body, realizing she can't see it. "All sexual stuff or I create life, not like pregnancy, but, like, magical, cursed by a god life? What if I get a Pap smear? Is my underwear going to start miraculously turning into people? Toilet paper? Sex toys? Condoms?"

She answers my questions indirectly: "You have to be the one to insert it. It has to reach at least 4.2 inches inside you. Also, it can't already be alive."

Wait, 'can't already be alive'? Does that mean it can be dead? Or does that just mean 'inanimate'?

"Unbelievable," I say, but my hands are cold, and my heart is playing a little drum solo in my chest.

"Are you mad at me?" she asks, softer.

"I don't know what I am," I say, unable to form a coherent thought.

CHAPTER 2
ALICE

I nearly overfill a glass with wine and drink it in one go.

It's not enough, but it's a start.

My apartment couldn't be described as neat by even the most charitable. It's a mess—aggressively so. It's a mostly open floor plan: living room spilling into dining room (aka home office), spilling into kitchen.

The kitchen, where I stand now, is the cleanest room in the house. It has that minimalistic flair you'd think was a style choice, but it really just means I don't cook. The only decorations are a garish fake plant and a row of takeout soy sauce packets lined up by height on the windowsill.

If I were hoping a little wine and a lot of sarcasm would exorcise my mother's words from my brain, I am a certified dumbass.

The silence in my apartment is bleak. It's that type of silence that feels like it reaches into your skull and scrapes out any last bit of sound waves that had the audacity to linger in there.

Restless, I move to my home office, open my laptop, and turn some music on—'lofi beats to study to'. Not that I'll be studying. I just can't stand the silence, and lyrics distract me from the important work of doing absolutely nothing.

The dining room consists of a card table I've deemed suitable for dining, but still just use to pile crap upon and my home office, which is just a desk. The desk is adorned with: two monitors; a laptop that has to be levitated, or it will melt a hole in the wood; a hole in the wood underneath it where I learned that; a peripheral keyboard and mouse; and a mug of coffee I made yesterday but forgot to finish—which, weirdly, feels like a win for me. *I was able to get through the day without a whole pot. Go me!*

I linger at the laptop, the potential Google search of "Midas vagina curse," feeling too heavy for my cellphone's browser. I can't decide whether to laugh, cry, Google, or booty-call an ex. In the end, I just sit perfectly still and listen to the 'lofi beats to have an existential crisis to', and stare into the abyss, thinking about what, precisely, would happen if I stuffed a stapler into my vagina.

"Ridiculous," I mutter, slapping the desk with unnecessary violence. But the image won't leave. The stapler is a sleek little number in brushed aluminum. *Would it come to life as a cold, fastidious accountant? A guy with wire-rim glasses and a strict no-nonsense policy on collating?*

I shake myself, close the laptop lid—which turns off the music—and march into the kitchen, daring myself not to think about the wine bottle sexually as I pour myself more wine.

The living room is decorated like I'm trying to terrify some hypothetical realtor or confuse any AI staging algorithm stupid enough to train on it. I have various knick-knacks and bric-à-brac scattered throughout with no discernible intention. You can't see most of it, though, considering it's all under piles of sorta clean clothes and definitely moldy takeout.

I flop onto my couch and seize the TV remote, turning it on with a flourish. A streaming crime drama is already queued up—an all-female cast of homicide detectives, every single one of them so sleep-deprived and hot that it's honestly distracting.

But not distracting enough…

My eyes drift to the remote lying motionless at my side—its shape eliciting illicit ideas about where I could shove it. *Would the remote come alive as a bland, channel-flipping dudebro? Or maybe he'd be a really controlling guy who seemed like a good deal at first, only to reveal his original personality was a sort of promotional bait-and-switch, and his package requires mandatory equipment rentals to function?*

I watch an entire episode but retain nothing. My mind keeps drifting. There's something sticky and weird about my thoughts—like my brain is hammocked in a spiderweb of perversion. I'm distracted by increasingly unhinged thoughts of literal fuckery.

I count the objects in my apartment that could be, in a hypothetical universe, the first thing to enter my nethers after midnight.

The number is alarmingly high. Everything looks phallic. Everything has a personality.

Even the large glass egg paperweight on my coffee table seems like something I could potentially push into my pussy. My brain conjures up a man made entirely of weird optical distortions, all refracted rainbows, shifting depths, and undiagnosed, unmedicated ADHD. He'd never stop moving, always restless, always bending light to suit himself.

My phone buzzes. It's a text from my mother:

MOM
Just remember, sweetie—midnight.

I don't respond. Instead, I type "hereditary magical vagina curse" into Google, but all I get are links to horror movies and urban legend forums. I consider all of my family's spouses and lovers and wonder how many of them were once objects. I laugh—actual laughter, because what else can you do? It's so fucking absurd.

My eye catches the time. It's 11:09. I should be winding down for bed, not entertaining my mom's ridiculous warning and definitely not making sexy eyes at the candlestick on the bookshelf beside my couch.

I stand, stretch, and move to my bedroom—an equally messy and equally depressing space attached to the living room. I toss my phone on the bed and wander to the bathroom. It's the only bathroom in the place. So, if I ever invite people over, they have to go through my bedroom to pee—it's annoying, and I hate it, but I'm too lazy to move and don't invite many people over anyway.

I make a face in the mirror: tongue out and eyes crossed. "You do not have a twat of transmutation or whatever," I inform my face. "You are not cursed. You are a mildly educated woman with a 401(k) and a negative net worth."

My face looks unconvinced.

On the counter, my electric toothbrush leans in its charger. I imagine shoving it up my cooch and having a pretty good time, actually. It becomes a man in dental scrubs, who vibrates with nervous energy, and we get along swimmingly—at first. He constantly harasses me to floss. I never do. We fight about it incessantly, only to break up after a year of couples therapy—our last meeting of which I selfishly cry, "Why do you insist on trying to change me?"

My hairbrush sits on the countertop next to it, equally phallic but less vibratey. I stare at it, then pick it up. I set it back down. Pick it up, set it down. "Nope," I say to it, as if it's trying to tempt me with its slutty little handle and pornographic bristles.

I'm losing it. I really am.

I brush my teeth (*with my potential future husband?*) and climb into bed.

My eyes roam the room, clocking every object that could even remotely fit inside me—those that couldn't naturally, I devise schemes around how I could. And, the most frustrating part of it all, is that it's making me horny as hell.

CHAPTER 3
ALICE

I'm hiding from the watchful eyes of all the objects in my room with the comforter pulled over my head.

I'm not sleeping anytime soon. That much is obvious. The anxious rumination of my mind has somehow translated to full-fledged, painful arousal. I absentmindedly pet my clit through my pajamas, thinking about the vibrator in my nightstand.

If this curse is real, I'll never be able to use it again. And that feels like a worse fate than turning it into some hottie with my high-tech vibrator attached to his crotch.

I pop out from under the covers to look at my alarm clock.

11:50.

I could get it done before midnight. It usually takes, like, three minutes. Maybe I should. One last hoo-ha hurrah before I have to retire it forever.

I sit on the edge of the bed and open the nightstand drawer. I have no reason to do this, but the idea is in my head now, so…

There it is—the closest thing I've had to a boyfriend in years—my vibrator. It's expensive, high-tech, and sits in its own travel case. The case lies open, since I never take the time to close it, on top of a million random objects that have no reason to be in the drawer other than I had them when I was in my room and needed a place to put them. The case cradles it like a precious artifact.

Let's say, for the sake of the argument, that I were to turn this thing into a human. *It would be the logical choice for a boyfriend, right? If I'm going to manifest a magical stalker from thin air, I might as well aim for someone with stamina, right?*

Would it remember all the times I've fucked it?

I consider it, as if interviewing it for a job. I giggle to myself and say to it, "So, why should I choose you as my life partner?" I turn it on and it hums as if answering, "Well, my strengths are stamina and my weaknesses are I am not dishwasher safe, but you don't have a dishwasher, so we're kind of made for each other."

I hold it in my palm, testing the weight. I run my thumb along the silicone ridge, as if the act of touching it might prove or disprove a theory. I consider putting it in, just as a fuck you to fate and family curses everywhere.

11:55.

Shit. I still have time, but if I were to use it now, I'd be risking it.

I eye it with the lasciviousness of a woman possessed. *How the fuck long is 4.2 inches, anyway? Maybe this thing isn't even that long, and I don't have to worry about it. I know that is extreme wishful thinking, but I'm gonna find out.*

Underneath the vibrator case, amongst the other random, unnecessary to have in my nightstand, crap is a ruler. It's 12 inches of fluorescent blue plastic, the kind you get as a kid and then just keep around forever in case of measuring emergencies.

I run my finger along the edge, nail catching on the 4-inch mark, then going to the fourth notch after that. *How do they know it's 4.2 inches? Why not 4.25? The ruler doesn't even show 4.2 inches.*

I hold it up to my eye level and examine the length.

That's not that long. Now I get why a tampon can cause trouble.

I think about the last time I used this ruler—and what ultimately led to it living inside my nightstand. I brought a one-night stand home. Some guy named Todd, I met at a bar, who said he was, and I quote, "hung like a literal ruler."

He wasn't.

He was closer to the 6-inch mark, which, to be fair, is above average—at least in my experience.

I bet this ruler would be hung like a ruler…literally.

I think about all the times I got myself off after a bad date, all the mornings I woke up sticky and sad, convinced it would be different next time. It never is.

I hold the ruler next to the vibrator: 5 inches.

Huh. Not even as long as Todd.

Maybe I should just fuck this ruler.

11:59.

I wish I could say I wasn't considering fucking this ruler. But…I'm considering fucking this ruler.

I want to prove my mother wrong. Get this idea out of my head once and for all. But…on the off-chance my mom isn't lying, I think I'd rather have the lover hung like a ruler.

I try to consider the potential personalities of the two objects in my hands, but really, I can't. My thoughts are driven by a kind of eff you to Todd and every other past male lover with an inflated ego and impulsivity that probably comes from a long line of ancestral stupidity.

12:00.

The clock ticks over with a flicker, and nothing in the world changes.

No magic ripple, no crackle of fate. I'm still me. I don't feel any different.

Nope. Just me, my vibrator, and this dumb plastic ruler, sitting here on the edge of the bed.

I put the vibrator back in its box and measure my fingers. The longest is 3 inches. *Not long enough.* I reach inside myself anyway to see if anything feels different in there.

Nope.

12:01.

I put my fingers at the 4.25 mark. I wonder how deep that feels.

I stare at the tick mark. There's a little mark there, faint and faded as if I had measured something 4.25 inches once.

I brace the ruler between my palms, like I'm making a little spit roast of idiocy, and stare at it. There's something about it. Something familiar.

Zero to twelve—clean and simple. No ambiguity. I like that about it. I like that if you measure something, you know exactly where it stands. People aren't like that. Ancient curses aren't like that. The gods who hand out curses pretending they are gifts aren't like that.

12:04.

Fuck it. I'm gonna fuck it.

I put my fingers at the 5-inch mark. *Might as well go a little deeper just in case.*

I slide off my pajama bottoms and panties, leaving them in a heap on the floor.

I lean back, spreading my legs, feeling equal parts doomed and dumb.

I bring the ruler to my opening and test it, gently, like I'm checking the temperature of bathwater. It's uncomfortable, but not sharp like I expect it to be.

I exhale and press it in further. There's a brief sting, but mostly just pressure. I push it in a little more, until the plastic disappears into the wet heat of me, and my fingers brace against my lips.

I feel nothing. Not even the cheap thrill I'd hoped for, just a persistent, medical kind of emptiness.

Will it just transform right here inside me? Will it explode into a complete human and break me into a million pieces, or would this just be, like, its dick or something?

Mom would have told me if I was in danger of exploding myself, right? I dunno, she didn't tell me about this supposed curse…

I hold the ruler in place, braced between two fingers at the 5-inch mark, and wait. Part of me expects a lightning strike, a monstrous throb of energy, or at least a minor hallucination. But there's only the sound of my breathing.

I stay like that for a minute, maybe two, trying to feel for a change.

Nothing happens.

I pull it out, awkward and wet, and now weirdly hornier and super annoyed about it. I look at the ruler, glistening in the light of my clock, and feel an anger and disappointment I wasn't prepared for.

My body feels hollow and foolish, my head full of static. A surge of anger overwhelms me. I never expected I'd spend the start of my twenty-seventh birthday crammed with disappointment and cheap plastic, waiting for the world to crack open and give me something to love.

I say to the ruler, "You're not even my boyfriend, and you're already disappointing me," as a ludicrous tear runs down my eye.

The ruler says nothing. Of course it doesn't.

CHAPTER 4
ALICE

There's no curse. I didn't inherit any magical vaginal abilities.

If I've inherited anything from the women in my family, it's a knack for self-sabotage and the inability to let go.

Maybe that's the real curse.

I stare at the ceiling and think about all the women in the world (in my family) who have disappointed themselves in this exact pose: wide-legged and hollow, waiting for a miracle.

Heat blooms behind my face as if the anger, unquenched arousal, and embarrassment are all trying to spill out of me at once.

I grab my pillow and smash it over my face, then scream into it. It feels dumb, but I do it again, louder. I guess I was more invested in the idea of having a devoted lover who was hung like a horse (*well, a ruler*) than I thought.

I toss the pillow aside, breathless from screaming. The ruler is on the bed, half-hidden under the sheets, and I glare at it like it's to blame for all of this.

I reach between my legs, hoping an orgasm will reset my brain and release this awful feeling that's built inside me.

I rub in tight, angry circles, not bothering with the gentle teasing lead-up I usually start with. My eyes are fixed on the ruler. I will myself to feel anything but shame, and I do: loneliness and fury.

I roll my hips, grinding into my palm, and think about all the men who have lied about their lengths. I imagine measuring them with the ruler, deeming them insufficient for my needs, and then rubbing one out in front of them while mocking their dicks. Then, after they leave, crying about how lonely I am.

My breath quickens, and I knead faster, harder, madder, sadder.

Then I imagine the ruler transforming into a tongue, a hand, a disembodied embodiment of devotion.

My core clenches, my fingers cramp, but I keep going, keep pushing, until the pressure finally breaks. The explosion of release is accompanied by a grunt and then a sigh.

I close my eyes, trying to bask in the afterglow, and feeling only marginally less disappointed. When my heart rate slows, I'm sweaty and sticky and prepped to resume my self-loathing spiral, reopening my eyes.

The ruler is glowing, casting a blue light so faint that I think my eyes are playing tricks on me. But the light grows stronger—undeniable—and the atmosphere shifts, leaving an emptiness in my head. A low, pounding thrum, like the building's water pipes about to burst, builds in volume, and the glow pulses to the rhythm. A weird scent curls up my nostrils—ozone and warm pennies and burning plastic.

What the actual fuck!?

My heart stops, and I swat the ruler away, sending it flying across the room to smack against the wall and land in a pile of theoretically clean clothes.

I'm hallucinating. It's the wine. The pent-up hormones. The intergenerational trauma.

The ruler IS NOT GLOWING.

But it is...

It's casting an increasing bright blue light, so blinding that I almost don't see the dark shadow expanding against the wall.

I scramble for the comforter, cover my bits, and squint, trying to see the center of the light source.

The ruler is...stretching? Growing into some weird, translucent jelly mass that wobbles and morphs. First, it looks a bit like a stick-figure, then, horrifyingly, a fully-formed man.

A very large, very naked, very hot man.

Then the glowing stops, so suddenly it's startling. It blips out all light, leaving me terrified, clinging my comforter to my chest, and unsure if I'm about to be attacked by some random hottie in the dark.

I don't let the darkness settle; I immediately turn on my bedside light. Then I scoot back into the corner my bed is pushed against, realizing I have only one exit, and he's standing right in front of it.

He's completely nude and not trying to hide it—though I don't know why he would. He's solid and chiseled, and perfectly symmetrical. And, I'm gonna be honest here, I see his dick before I even see his face. It's huge. Long. Swinging with the same architectural precision as the rest of him. Then I see his face: the perfect approximation of everything perfect, all existing neatly under expertly tousled black hair.

My mouth goes dry. I try to speak, but the only sound that comes out is a high, wheezy cough.

The apparition opens his eyes, and they flicker with the same glacial blue that once colored the ruler. "Are you okay?" he asks, voice low and careful, as if testing vocal cords for the first time.

I clutch the comforter tighter and scoot even more into the corner, attempting to meld my body with the drywall. "Who are you? How did you get here?"

He inclines his head the smallest degree. "I am Gage. You summoned me."

"I wha?" I ask, unable to form words with more than three letters.

He steps forward, and every movement is fluid, measured, beautiful. "You put me inside you." He says with zero humor, as if stating a legal fact. "That act constitutes summoning."

My brain flips through about fifty responses and settles on, "Are you…the ruler?"

His lips twitch, almost a smile. "I was. Now I am Gage, G-A-G-E." His eyes linger on mine, gentle, unblinking, impossibly blue. "My purpose is to measure up. I am deeply sorry for the earlier disappointment."

I want to die. I want to melt through the mattress. I want to stop stealing glances at his dick, but it's impossible. I want to reply and not sound like someone stupid enough to push a ruler into her puss, but that's also impossible, because I say, "You're naked. And you're in my apartment."

He looks down, as if noticing his own nudity for the first time. He shrugs, perfectly at ease. "I can remedy that if it offends you. But my understanding is that this is customary, given the nature of our transaction."

Holy fuck, my mom wasn't lying.

The curse, the transformation, the lifelong threat of bad decisions and weaponized sexuality—it's all real. And standing in my bedroom, currently staring at me as if I'm the one who just materialized out of thin air, is the literal manifestation of my most impulsive decision ever.

I don't know whether to laugh or scream.

"So what happens now?" I ask, through shaking breath.

Gage sits on the edge of the bed, leaving a chivalrous distance. "I am at your disposal," he says. "I exist to satisfy your requirements. I have a comprehensive knowledge of your sexual preferences, as recorded during my tenure in the nightstand."

This is too much.

"This isn't possible," I whisper. "You're not real."

"I am real, Alice. I am here for you."

I gulp. "Okay. Let's say you are real. You're...what...my magical sex golem?"

He nods. "That is an acceptable term. Technically, I am a physical manifestation of your intent, shaped by your subconscious and the mechanics of the hereditary enchantment."

I can't help it—I giggle a little hysterically. "And you're here to... satisfy my requirements?"

Gage inclines his head. "Correct. I reviewed your previous complaints regarding men and made the appropriate adjustments to my form."

I study him, looking for signs of a joke, a trick, anything that would make this less terrifying, but he's just sitting there, patient and poised. I ask, "Adjustments?"

"I witnessed your disappointment with Todd. I ensured my form would not provoke the same reaction."

I try to think of a clever retort, something self-deprecating or urbane, but all I can manage is, "So…you have a foot-long dick?"

He looks down at himself, shrugs. "That was the specification he failed to meet that led to your disappointment."

I bark out a laugh, short and wild. "Jesus, you're literal."

"That is also true," he says, with just the faintest hint of pride.

I reach out, tentative, and poke his arm. It's solid, the way you want a body to be.

He waits, silent and still, until I meet his eyes.

"You're really here?" I ask.

He nods, solemn. "I am here. I am yours."

CHAPTER 5
ALICE

Gage moves closer, resting his weight on his palm, but not crowding me. I don't back away, but I also don't drop the comforter still clenched under my chin.

"May I touch you?" he asks, as politely as someone asking for the salt.

A dozen sarcastic quips die in my throat. Instead, I just stare at him, feeling my pulse thumping in my neck.

I should be terrified. I should call the police, or an exorcist, or my mother.

Instead, fool that I am, I mutter, "Okay."

He smiles and places his hand on my leg over the comforter. We both stare where his hand meets my leg for a long moment. Then he looks directly at my face, and our eyes lock. There is so much sincerity behind the uncanny perfection when he says, "Thank you."

"For what?"

"For giving me hands with which I may touch you."

"Umm…you're welcome."

With his other hand, he slowly reaches for the edge of the comforter, where I grip it at my throat. "But will you let me touch you unobstructed? Now that I have flesh, it is my greatest wish to feel the softness of yours against it."

For a moment, I'm speechless. Not just because of the absurdity, but because it might be the sweetest thing anyone has ever said to me.

"Umm…okay," I say, meek and soft, still not believing this is happening.

Gage takes the blanket from my grip and drags it to the side, exposing my body, naked from the waist down. He points at the edge of my shirt. He doesn't need to ask; I understand and nod. He lifts it over my head.

His eyes widen as he takes me in. They don't roam like other men's; they scan, catalog, calculate, and measure, as if he is both impressed by me and a little perplexed.

He tentatively places his hand on my shin, then slides up with slow dedication, as if mapping my leg and recording every detail—tracing every muscle, every tendon. His touch is so exact, so deeply attentive, it drops most of my usual defenses. "Fascinating," he murmurs.

When he reaches my thigh, I tense, ticklishness and modesty overriding my calm. He stops. "May I continue?"

I nod, and he continues his trek upward until he presses his thumb into the divot near my hip. "Your femur-to-pelvis ratio is ideal for your height class."

I bark out a laugh. "Is that a good thing?"

His hand never leaves my skin. "Oh, yes. Your leg is quantifiably, undeniably perfect. I look forward to measuring the rest of you."

Something in my chest twists. It's not just arousal, though that's rolling in hot waves up my belly; it's the weird delight of being worshipped.

His other hand joins the first, and now he's using both palms to measure the width of my hips, the swell of my ass, the curve of my waist.

He keeps up a low commentary, more to himself than to me. I catch words like "circumference," "mean," "optimal," "distribution," and "angle."

I want to say something snide, but every word melts before it gets out.

His hands move up, slowly, cupping my ribs, tracing each one with artistic reverence.

When he gets to my breasts, he pauses for just a moment, waiting for my response. I just close my eyes and bite my lip in anticipation.

He cups me with both hands, weighing each breast. His thumbs brush over my nipples, hardening them instantly. "Turgor response is immediate," he notes, almost in awe. "That's very good."

I laugh. "Are you benchmarking me?"

"No. That would imply I was trying to improve you, which I am not. 'Calibrating' is more accurate."

"What's the difference?"

"I am collecting measurements to ensure I will never disappoint you again."

Gage leans forward and kisses the inside of my knee. Then inches his way up, with gentle, slow kisses. When he reaches the meat of my thigh, he pauses.

He pushes my legs apart and grins, eyes locked on my widespread lips, as he settles between my thighs. He doesn't dive in—no, he studies, taking a complete visual inventory. He's so close, I can feel him there, but I stay frozen, the anticipation of his proximity keeping me in place.

Then, he gently traces my folds, circling my clit, making my walls flutter.

"You are very wet," he observes, a trace of wonder in his voice.

"Your calibrations meet my specifications," I whisper, trying to speak his dorky language.

He presses two fingers inside me, and the pressure is so perfect it pushes a deep moan out of me. He grins, pleased with himself, and works them inside me. They're slender, impossibly deft, and know precisely where to curl and just how far to push—as if they were designed specifically with my pussy in mind—and, I suppose, since he said he is a manifestation of my desires, they were.

He draws slow, perfect circles against my clit with his thumb, and it's like every nerve in my body wakes up at once.

He leans forward, replacing his thumb with the tip of his tongue. He drags it in slow, desperate circles, as if thoroughly tasting me. He locks eyes with my face, watching my reaction, cataloguing every shiver and gasp with obsessive attention.

Usually, when someone goes down on me, I can't look—mortified by the vulnerability of the whole thing—but, with him, I can't look away. He makes me feel like a goddess, like he's worshiping at the altar of my body. And, best of all, the way he looks at me makes me feel like I actually deserve this level of attention. His gaze is so earnest, so unguarded, I can't help but believe he's enjoying himself.

He brings me to the edge fast, too fast, and I try to slow him down, to savor the moment, but I suspect Gage is the type of man who doesn't allow for inefficiency. When I come, I do so with a startled yelp, bucking my hips so violently he has to hold my legs so I don't kick him in the face.

The aftershocks are wild and long, like a guitar string plucked too hard and followed by one of those skin-crawl-inducing whammy bar things.

Gage does not stop. He applies measured pressure, coaxing another wave and then another, until my brain is just static and wet heat.

When he finally lets up, he crawls up the bed and pulls me into his arms. "Did I hurt you?" he asks, brushing my hair back.

I shake my head, still dazed. "No. That was…" I can't finish the sentence, so I just lie there, panting.

Gage holds me for a long minute, then lifts my chin so I have to meet his eyes. "Then may I continue?"

I nod. Words are gone.

CHAPTER 6
ALICE

Gage pulls my legs forward, lying me flat on my back, then hovers over me, lining his cock up with my entrance.

I look at his dick, and it's absurd. Not monstrous, not cartoonish—just a foot of perfect, symmetrical cock, lightly veined and flushed. It's as if a math prodigy custom-ordered it for aesthetics and function, and then doubled it just in case.

"Is that…" I gesture at him, then my own body. "Is it supposed to fit?"

He gives a tiny shrug. "My calibrations indicate it should."

I snort, and suddenly the fear is gone, replaced by a greedy sort of curiosity. "Show me, then."

It's intimidating, but Gage takes his time, easing in centimeter by perfect centimeter. He watches my face the whole time, checking for even a hint of pain.

It doesn't hurt. Somehow, it fits—he was telling the truth.

I gasp when he bottoms out, a stretch that borders on sublime, and he stays there, pulsing gently, until my body stops clenching and starts begging for more.

He sets a rhythm, deep and slow at first, and accelerating as I adjust. Every thrust is deliberate, mathematically optimal. He changes angles just so, testing the architecture of my insides, until he finds the vector that makes me cry out, high and helpless.

"You're incredible," he whispers, sweat beading on his perfect brow. "Thank you for giving me this body so that I may experience this."

I want to tell him that he's the incredible one, that I've never been fucked like this, but the words get lost in the surge.

Every motion, every sound, every measured increase in pressure is designed to unravel me.

His hands are everywhere: charting the length of my spine, the span of my ribs, the hypersensitive slope behind my ear.

Gage keeps up his cataloguing, too, murmuring a constant stream of data to himself: "Temperature spike…contractions…seven seconds…" He's fascinated, obsessed, delighted by every new metric.

Raw, unvarnished flattery punctuates the measurements: "You are so, so beautiful…perfect in every measurable way…quantifiably flawless…"

His praise hits me harder than his dick.

Gage brings me to the edge over and over. I lose count of the orgasms. It's just a rolling continuum of pleasure, cresting and receding, punctuated by his quiet, reverent affirmations.

There's a point where the body stops being a thing you pilot and becomes a thing that pilots you. It feels more like being possessed by your own nerves, every circuit overloaded and arcing. Gage brings me to that threshold and then shoves me through it—over and over until I'm not even sure where I end and he begins.

I'm coming down from an orgasm, and I feel like that gooey substance Gage was right before he became a fully fleshed-out human. He flips me onto my stomach and slides in from behind. He keeps one palm splayed between my shoulder blades, pinning me with just enough force that my weightless body won't float away.

He sets a tempo that's fast, remorseless, and absolutely relentless.

I arch, toes curling against the sheets.

I can no longer speak. Every sound comes out as a gasp or a helpless whine.

Gage kisses the back of my neck.

Then, unfathomably, he increases his pace. His hips slap against me, each beautifully brutal thrust forcing my breath from my lungs.

"You are perfect," he growls, and the sincerity in his voice unravels me.

I claw at the sheets, desperate for something to anchor me. I'm convinced my soul is leaving my body.

My legs shake, and Gage wraps his arms around me, holding me steady through the storm. He doesn't stop, not even when I scream.

Especially not then.

He slows, eventually, but even his slow is more than most men's sprint.

He keeps me right on the brink of delirium, milking every spasm out of me until my body sags, exhausted and grateful.

At one point, I think he's done, finally exhausted himself. He rolls us onto our sides, spooning me close, and runs a fingertip along my temple.

My vision blurs. The room spins. My heart pounds so loud I think it might burst.

"Are you still with me?" he murmurs.

I try to answer, but all I can manage is a tremulous laugh. "I think you broke me."

"You do not appear broken," he says, concern contorting his face. "Is it internal?" He looks over my body with a panicked gaze.

"It's a saying. It's a good thing," I say, with a giggle.

He sighs with relief, and his smile returns.

Gage shifts, pressing his miraculously still hard dick behind me, while nudging my thighs apart. He asks, "Since you are not broken, shall I continue?"

I think I might die, but it seems like a good way to go, so I say, "Okay."

The pleasure continues, and it could be seconds, it could be minutes. I'm so lost to all of it; I think I might have entirely lost my mind.

After this whole time, Gage hasn't come, but he finally comes with a grunt and a shudder, filling me so full I swear I can feel him in my diaphragm.

His orgasm triggers another in me, and this one hits me like a blackout. My body goes rigid, then limp, every synapse short-circuited. My vision tunnels to pure blue, brighter than the ruler ever was, until I see nothing but stars.

My final coherent thought, before everything winks out, is that my mother was right—about the curse, about the magic, about the need to choose wisely. I've never chosen anything wisely—ever. But my brain is exploding like the last panel on the exploding brain meme, so this must have been a wise choice after all.

He collapses beside me, still holding me, and strokes my back in slow, calming circles.

"You're amazing," I say as the soft darkness of my mind envelops me.

He brushes my hair from my forehead, tucks the blankets around me, and leans in until his lips are a breath away from my ear. He whispers, "Then I have served my purpose."

I want to ask him what he means by that, but I drift off before I can.

I dream of blue light and measuring tapes and the wild, miraculous feel of being known to the inch.

CHAPTER 7
GAGE

I could watch her forever. In fact, I think I will. It's my life's purpose, after all—at least until she wakes and tells me what to do instead.

She's on her stomach, arms thrown above her head. Her hair is a coppery sprawl across the pillow, and strands snare in the damp sweat on her forehead. Her breathing is slow and reliable—each inhale is a precise 3.1 seconds, each exhale a slightly longer 3.3 seconds.

Alice: creator, lover, subject and object, goddess, sleeper.

Perfect. Everything.

My everything.

My reason for being—literally and figuratively.

The skin on her shoulder is pale and freckled. The curve of it arcs out from under the edge of the comforter with perfect continuity. The blanket only covers half her ass. This is, mathematically, the optimal amount for viewing.

I drift my palm over her back, tracing every vertebra—committing every curve to memory. Once I feel I've thoroughly measured her back, I withdraw my hand to study it.

I flex my new fingers, watching the knuckles ripple. I splay them, palm up, and the sensation is so detailed it's almost violent.

The mirror over her dresser catches my attention; the person in the glass is unfamiliar, but obviously me.

Every part of my body is still learning how to exist; each step is a test to see if my body works the way I think it should. I slide out of bed, careful not to disturb her. She makes a sound and I freeze. But it's just a dream-sigh. She doesn't wake.

I walk to the mirror, reviewing my reflection. I flex my biceps, which I know is a cliché, but this is my first time in front of a mirror, so I am permitted such vanity at the moment. I check the proportions of my chest, abs, and thighs.

The ridiculous length of cock currently hanging like a trophy between my thighs is sticky, heavy, swollen. It's 8.6 inches in its current state, but precisely a foot long when filled with blood—meeting her exact specifications.

When Alice's eyes first fell on this form of mine, there was fear, then hunger, then desire. My mouth tugs into what I understand is a grin at the memory of using this thing to please her. When I got hard for her, the sensation of blood surging into a space that hadn't existed mere minutes before was terrifying and beautiful. Then she opened for me, cautious at first and then desperate.

Back when I was a ruler, she put me up against the dick of a man she brought home: Todd. Her mouth turned down at the corners, and she said, "Well, that's not what you promised," when I proved he didn't match his boast—not even close—only 6 inches. I, however, stood proud, tall, a foot—measuring up to her expectations.

His face fell in embarrassment, but his dick didn't. He spent the next 37 minutes lying to her about other things in hopes she'd sleep with him. The whole time, she stroked me absentmindedly. After he finally left, she was so unsatisfied sexually she had to use that obnoxious vibrator to relieve herself in a way Todd apparently couldn't—in a way I never could until now.

Now, here I am: the full 12 inches of me, designed to specification, optimized for her pleasure.

I feel a fluttering in my chest, so I place my palm flat on it. A pounding raises my hand slightly, and for 1.2 seconds, I worry something is malfunctioning, then realize it's just my heart beating, and it's supposed to do that—at least, I think it is.

I look down at Alice's bare back, and something strange stirs in me: a need to protect, to prove my worth, to be indispensable. The thought is both horrifying and lovely.

I scan the rest of the bedroom, eyes cataloguing every object she could have chosen instead of me. The feeling that follows is not victory, exactly, but something like relief.

I think about the ruler I was—am, in some deep quantum sense. That entire existence feels so long ago. Feels unreal. Flat, and not just because I was literally flat.

I have all the memories: being shrink-wrapped with my five brothers; standing proudly in a pencil cup in Alice's third-grade classroom; tucked behind a row of books for 3.6 months, collecting dust; and squeezed next to a fun-loving sharpie and an ornery pair of scissors in a junk drawer.

But the best memories are from living in her nightstand; all previous years as a 12-inch stick of fluorescent blue plastic were just a tragic prelude.

I open the drawer where I lived for years. Staring back at me is the sleek vibrator, sitting in its custom-molded cradle, pompous in its ability to bring her pleasure.

I study it for a moment. I pick it up and turn it around, feeling the perfect balance, the minimalist lines, the measly 5 inches. If this thing ever walked upright, it would be an arrogant, tailored-suited man, the kind who writes self-help books and never once doubts his own perfection.

"She didn't pick you, after all," I whisper, turning the vibrator over. "She picked me."

It's not rational, this spike of jealousy.

Still, the vibrator's silence is smug.

I imagine it sneering at me, the way only an object with a single job can sneer. I place it back in the drawer, just a little off-center, to let it know who's boss. The vibrator waits, patient, knowing if it's ever called upon, it will do its job with ruthless efficiency. I lean in close and whisper, "You'll never be enough." And for a moment, I'm not sure who I'm trying to convince.

I close the drawer and return my attention to Alice.

Last night, I saw her face when she realized how literal I was. It made her laugh, which triggered a corresponding impulse in me—laughter as both a contagion and a reward.

I'd never experienced pleasure before. The closest thing was when she'd slap me against her palm, but that was just sensation, not emotion. But fucking her, it was both at once, fused together and amplified by the fact I was with her.

I look over at her now, breathing deep and even, and the urge to wake her up just to do it all again is so strong I have to physically restrain myself.

Instead, I watch her and count the freckles on her back.

I vow to never let her down. To always be what she needs.

I will make her happy. Happier than any vibrator or lover ever has.

Her happiness will be the measure by which I judge my own existence. I will organize her life and anticipate her needs before she even knows them. I will be indispensable.

I realize this is not love as people describe it, but then again, I am not people. I am a ruler, recalibrated and promoted to a "sex golem" as she called me.

But I will be more than that.

"I will measure up to everything you need," I whisper, and the phrase sends a pulse through my whole body.

I know I am lucky. Blessed—if you believe in such things.

Of all the objects in this apartment, I was the one chosen, the one transformed. She gave me this: sight, touch, the ability to want.

But I also remember what it's like to be left behind. To be set aside for months, years, only to be used when needed, and then be shoved back into darkness. I remember the shock of the junk drawer, the taste of lint and graphite and dead batteries. I remember Alice's date, the one who measured himself against me and came up short, never to be seen again.

Those memories float within me like a warning.

I will not be set aside. Not by her. Not again.

I will not come up short.

I close my eyes and run through all the ways I can make her life better.

CHAPTER 8
ALICE

I wake slowly, each sense coming to me at a leisurely pace, intermixed within my dreams.

Every inch of my body hurts, in the good way, like I ran a marathon and celebrated by getting hit by a bag of dicks. Something inside me is empty and raw and humming, like I have a subwoofer installed in my uterus. There's a sore spot on my hipbone that feels precisely like the imprint of an obsessed man's palm.

I can still taste him. My mouth is dry, but there's a memory of something—ozone, graphite, and maybe a hint of blue raspberry popsicle.

I peel open an eye, and sun splinters through a slit in my blackout curtains, blinding me momentarily.

I'm alone.

The other half of the bed, which should be rumpled and warm, is pristine and cold. It looks like no one ever touched it.

Of course, it wasn't real. Of course, I didn't fuck a literal ruler who came to life and spent hours recalibrating my internal geometry.

It was a dream.

It was a feverish, wine-induced hallucination, starring my own neuroses and a psychosexual manifestation built out of middle-school nostalgia and desperation.

You aren't feeling the effects of a deep dicking; you're just hungover and probably masturbated yourself to sleep.

I prop myself up, clutching the comforter to my chest. The headache is already coming on, a thin band squeezing just above my eyebrows. I close my eyes, try to summon a calming mantra, but all I get is an intrusive replay of Gage's face murmuring, "You are so, so beautiful."

I don't even believe my own brain's propaganda.

I shuffle to the bathroom and check myself in the mirror, bracing for signs of supernatural tampering. I find only bedhead and smeared eyeliner, the universal sign of a woman who has given up on life.

I pee. The soreness feels less like an injury and more like a love note written in bruises. With my elbows atop my thighs, I place my head in my hands and try to piece together how much of last night was memory and how much was wishful thinking.

There's a thunk. Then another.

Muffled but distinct, coming from the direction of the living room.

I freeze midstream and listen.

The sound is slow and heavy. Followed by a slithering noise, like a measuring tape being pulled out and allowed to snap back in.

It's him. He's real.

I rush through the process of this peeing and hand-washing business and fuss with my appearance in the mirror just long enough to look less crazed. I dash to my bedroom to put on something more presentable, except I don't really have anything more presentable. Unfortunately, my wardrobe can be described as 'casual chic sans chic.' I look for my favorite sweatpants, but they're not in the dirty pile or in the "maybe clean" heap, so I settle for my college hoodie and a pair of novelty boxers with cats in space helmets.

The sounds are louder now, and accompanied by a low, steady muttering.

I push open the door, and the sight nearly short-circuits my brain.

Gage is standing in the middle of my now clean living room, totally naked, utterly at ease, and measuring the coffee table with a tape measure. He's so focused on the measurement that he doesn't notice me at first.

He reads out a number, then carefully writes something in a battered spiral notebook he must have found on my bookshelf. He moves on to the bookshelf itself, extending the tape upward, the metal tip clicking against the top. "One hundred seventy-five point six centimeters."

In the light of my living room, I get an eyeful of exactly how beautiful he is. He's perfectly proportioned, and every single muscle is somehow outlined by shadow, despite the bright light.

My eyes travel downward because I'm not made of stone.

The man's cock is as marvelous as I remember. It bobs with every shift of his posture. He seems completely unbothered by this, as if being a sexed-up carpenter is a perfectly natural thing to be.

He turns, catches sight of me, and his face lights up with instant, unfiltered joy.

"Alice," he says. "You're awake. Good." He nods approval, then goes back to the task at hand: measuring the distance between my couch cushions and noting it with a satisfied sigh.

I stand frozen and stare at him.

My brain tries to crash. Instead, it restarts.

Last night wasn't a dream. Or if it was, I'm still in it.

I open my mouth. I try to say something witty, or at least normal. What comes out is, "You're real."

He smiles, bashful and proud, like a puppy that just brought me my shoe. "Yes," he says. "And I'm here for you. Always."

"Holy fuck. I need to call my mom."

CHAPTER 9
ALICE

She picks up halfway through the first jangle, her voice instantly both soothing and accusatory: "You tried it, didn't you?"

I groan. "Hi, Mom."

She makes a pleased little grunt. "Don't play dumb, Alice. Everyone tries it before noon."

Gage stands next to me, working on my bookshelf, aligning each novel by height, then by color, then by "thematic resonance" (his phrase, not mine).

I sag into the couch, phone pinched between cheek and shoulder, and glare at my ceiling. "Yeah—"

There's a faint metallic clatter on her end—she's either doing the dishes or starting a garage band. She asks, "So, what did you use? Knowing you, it was a wine bottle."

I squeeze my eyes shut and try to will myself into a different timeline. "Mom, this is humiliating."

She cackles, delighted. "Oh, sweetie, it's only humiliating the first time. After that, you choose more wisely. Tell me." She says that assuming I'm humiliated about my choice of object, not my choice to shove an object up my puss or my choice to call my mom and talk about it.

Gage has resumed his project of measuring everything in my house with the single-mindedness of an Olympic athlete and the social awareness of a wet rock. I don't know where he got the tape measure, but it makes a satisfying-to-him, startling-to-me snap every time he retracts it.

It's a kind of performance art, watching him move around the living room. The way he leans over to get a perfect line of sight, all muscle and precision, would be a gift to anyone with a pulse and an Instagram account. He doesn't bother to hide anything, and even when he squats to read a measurement at floor level, his posture is elegant, deliberate—completely at odds with the absolute lunacy of the situation.

I can't believe I'm about to admit this to my mother. I mouth the words "kill me" at the ceiling, then mutter, "It was a ruler. His name is Gage."

"A ruler," she says. "Why?"

I hesitate, not ready to tell her the whole reason and not entirely sure myself, so I give her the half-truth. "I dunno. I was obsessed with what you said about the 4.2 inches."

Now she's openly giggling. "And how is he?"

I'm not sure if she's asking physiologically, sexually, or, like, around the house, but the answer is the same regardless. "Functional," I manage. "Thorough. Very…precise."

"Hold on, darling." She makes a happy noise. "Abby-baby, she chose a ruler! His name is Gage."

"I knew my daughter would pick something with numbers," a muffled male voice in the background exclaims—my father—the calculator watch, whose name is Abacus.

Oh, my God, it's so obvious. My eyes roll so far behind my head that I almost see the grey, gooey mass of my melted brain.

The muffled male voice now comes in deep, clear, and loud, as if he's standing behind my mom, yelling into the phone, "Hi, honey! I'm so happy for you. I can't wait to meet Gage!"

Mom huffs. "You don't have to yell; here, let me put it on speaker."

Dad always does this: hangs out in the periphery, trying to join in on our conversation, pretending not to be part of it, until they finally give up and just go on speakerphone.

"Hi, Dad," I say.

"Don't you have to be at work in forty-eight minutes?" he asks, ever the time keeper. *So fucking obvious now.*

"Yeah, Dad, it's fine. I work from home."

Mom chides. "Abby, don't derail."

I can practically hear my dad's stoic nod through the phone.

Gage is standing on a kitchen chair, using a laser pointer and a tape measure to map the exact distance between my ceiling fan and the nearest smoke detector. *I need to get him some clothes.* He catches me staring, smiles, and returns to work.

"So are…are all the men in our family ex-objects?"

"Pretty much," she laughs. "Either you were born from us or…born from us, if you get my drift. But it's not always a man. You can make any gender, really. It depends on what you're fantasizing about at the time."

Dad adds, "We're a physical manifestation of whatever you find most sexually attractive at the time."

I groan and flop backwards, feet kicking the opposite armrest. "Oh, my God. This is so embarrassing to talk to y'all about."

My mom chimes in: "There's nothing to be ashamed of. All the women in this family did the same thing. We're responsible for creating some of the best and weirdest men in the world."

"I'm so confused. How do all of them, like, just live normal lives in a world that documents and collects data on us since birth? Like, the government doesn't notice all these brand new people materializing from thin air?"

Dad grunts. "We're beings blessed by a god. We come with all the accessories we need to perform our functions."

Mom giggles. "Yeah, about a week after I made your dad, we found his accounting degree framed under my bed with a driver's license and social security card on top."

I giggle, then clamp a hand over my mouth. "This is the weirdest thing I've ever heard."

Mom continues, "Your cousin Ansley's husband, the divorce lawyer, he was a wedding cake knife, anyway, he came with a degree from Yale and Harvard! Can you believe it?"

Oh, my God, I hope she used the handle.

I look back at Gage. He crosses to the window and measures the distance between the sills, then the thickness of the glass, writing each figure down in the notebook. He stops, studies the page, then scribbles a note in the margin.

I duck into the bedroom, not wanting Gage to overhear me. I shut the door quietly behind me.

"Mom," I say, "can I ask you something serious?"

She replies. "Of course, honey."

Dad catches the hint. "I'm going to go finish the taxes. Love you, sweetie." I hear him kiss my mother.

"Love you, too," I say, not pointing out that tax season isn't for months.

Mom asks, "What is it, honey?"

"Is it permanent?" I ask. The words taste like a dare.

"Yeah, they can't return to their original forms," she admits. "He's not going to turn back to a ruler if you get him wet or anything." She giggles, and I've never heard her so happy before. It's like this secret has revealed a new side of her to me.

I ask, "No, I mean, like, is he always going to be…with me?"

"Well, it's just like any relationship," she says, and for the first time, her voice is gentle, almost sad. "They'll always love you, but they can certainly get fed up with your shit and leave. Some leave, go live new lives, but most just…become a part of the family. You'll see."

"But, what if I want out?" I squeeze the pillow, fingers going numb.

I think maybe I hear a pause in the snap of the measuring tape.

She drops her voice to a faux-whisper. "I mentioned your father wasn't my first, right? My first was a Ken doll."

I choke. "You're lying."

"Why would I lie about that?" She tsks, affronted. "Anyway, he was a nice man, but…we just weren't a good fit for either of us. It worked out in the end, though. He's living a good life. He's an actor-slash-director now. And I chose an object that better fits my personality. Your father is a prince, and he can bench-press me with one arm." She laughs.

I shudder. "Mom, please stop."

I let the silence stretch for a long time, then ask, "So, what am I supposed to do with him?"

"Feed him. Love him. Let him take care of you." She sounds like she's reading from a manual for a goldfish. "Oh, and don't be mean. They're loyal, but if you ignore them, they get weird. Your grandmother's first was a fountain pen, and he wrote passive-aggressive poetry for twenty years."

I fidget with the fraying edge of my comforter. The polyester threads catch under my fingernail and snap.

Mom sighs. "You don't have to do anything you don't want, Alice. But understand, they imprint. On you. Not like werewolf imprinting, but…" She lets it hang.

"But?" I prompt.

"They love you. In their way." There's a wobble in her voice, like she's skirting the edge of a sad memory. "It's not normal. It's intense. He'll adapt, but only if you treat him like a person and not an…object. Just be careful. Don't use him to hurt yourself or anyone else. They can't help but do what you want."

I glance at my bedroom door. Gage is out there, measuring. I can almost feel his attention radiating through the wall.

"So I'm responsible for him, forever? What if I mess it up? What if he gets bored, or angry, or turns into a serial killer?"

She laughs, but it's a tired sound. "They don't go bad, honey. They get weird. They get lonely. What's he doing now?"

I answer, "He's reorganizing my apartment and measuring everything."

"That's good! Let him! They crave purpose," Mom exclaims. "When I first made Ken, he racked up a ton of debt watching the home shopping network, buying all these weird clothes. He needed something to do. I got him a camcorder, and he started making all these artsy stop-motion movies with toys—all about me. Anyway, you have to let them help, darling. They get restless, otherwise."

She's silent for so long, I think the call dropped, but then: "Give it some time, sweetie. I bet you chose wisely."

I swallow, mouth gone dry. "You mean I'll love him."

"Probably." Her voice drops, a tremor under the calm.

I rub my forehead, squinting at the patterns of dust on my nightstand. "So that's it. This is my life now."

She tries to reassure me. "Listen, Alice. It is a literal gift from a god. Dionysus felt bad when King Midas turned his daughter into gold, so he gave all the other female descendants this gift. The gods didn't feel guilty often back then, so we should all feel quite blessed. It's only a curse if you view it that way."

CHAPTER 10
GAGE

I didn't hear everything she said. I wasn't trying to eavesdrop. But these ears apparently work on their own accord.

She said, "What if I want out?"

I measure the coffee table again, even though I already know it's 43 inches long, 2 feet wide, and 17.5 inches high. I try to focus on the numbers, let them crowd out the noise in my head, but Alice's voice keeps coming back.

I review the diagram I've created of her (our?) apartment, every measurement annotated and cross-checked, with areas for improvement noted.

I grip the notebook so tightly that the metal of the spiral digs deep into my hand. What I now know to be pain bites my fingers. I loosen my grip and the notebook falls to the ground. The metal dug so deeply into my hand, leaving red marks. For a second, I stare at the marks, fascinated.

The notebook lies open on the rug.

I bend to pick it up, but my fingers are clumsy. My body is still so new. It doesn't quite fit.

There are no instructions for me.

Alice made me with a ruler and a wish, and now I'm here, and it's my job to make her happy. That is all I know. My whole purpose is to satisfy.

I flip to my life's purpose.

MY LIFE'S PURPOSE: TO PLEASE AND CARE FOR ALICE.

<u>HOW TO FULFILL MY LIFE'S PURPOSE:</u>

1. BE USEFUL. CLEAN APARTMENT, COOK MEALS, FIX WHATEVER SHE BREAKS.

2. BE FUN. MAKE HER LAUGH, WATCH HER SHOWS, PLAY THE GAMES SHE LIKES.

<u>3. BE FUCKABLE. (IMPORTANT!!!)</u>

A) RESEARCH ANGLES AND POSITIONS FOR MAX PLEASURE

B) ASK FOR FEEDBACK (BUT NOT TOO MUCH)

C) GO SLOW UNLESS SHE SAYS OTHERWISE

I underline the third one, hard enough to crease the page. My hands are still shaking.

Alice made me to spec, but she didn't specify a purpose beyond the obvious.

Have I been focusing on the wrong thing?

I sit down on the floor, cross-legged, and stare at my dick.

Is this all she wants me for? Does she regret me already? Am I just a phase? A toy to be thrown away when she's done playing?

While she slept, I studied. I diagrammed what I learned from our night of intercourse: positions, angles, the vector of thrust, and the optimal speed for each phase. I cross-reference it with porn—some of it is pretty rough, but most of it is slower, focused, intimate.

I researched other ways to please her and take care of her, non-sexual ways, but for the last hour, I have been focused on cleaning and optimizing the apartment.

My chest tightens. Not in a physical way, but in a way that makes me want to tear open the walls and scream. I don't, because Alice hates noise. But I want to.

I try to picture what it would be like if she got rid of me.

Would I disappear? Shrink back into the ruler, plastic and hollow and forgotten in the drawer? Or would I just be alone, in the apartment, waiting for her to come home, counting the seconds like a prisoner?

I want to never leave. I want her to need me the way I need her—desperate and total, no air between us.

I can do better. I have to do better.

At the top of the first page, I write:

MUST NOT DISAPPOINT HER. IF SHE LEAVES, I WILL BE NOTHING.

I flip to a new page and begin to write the things that I know she likes.

I have existed in her presence for a long time, and now I can actually do something with the knowledge I have gained.

A LIST OF THINGS ALICE LIKES:

- **COFFEE, EXTRA STRONG, WITH 2.3 TABLESPOONS OF CREAMER**
- **CATS (ESPECIALLY WHEN PRINTED ON SHORTS—I LIKE THAT, TOO—A LOT)**
- **OBJECTS THAT ARE CUTE AND ALSO FUNCTIONAL (I, MYSELF, QUALIFY FOR AT LEAST TWO-THIRDS OF THAT, AS I AM NO LONGER AN OBJECT, BUT I THINK SHE FINDS ME CUTE.)**
- **TV SHOWS ABOUT MURDER, BUT ONLY IF THE DETECTIVES ARE WOMEN AND WEAR LOW-CUT SHIRTS**
- **LISTENING TO 'LOFI BEATS TO STUDY TO', WHILE NOT STUDYING**
- **NOT STUDYING**
- **WINE**

I continue writing until I have an exhaustive list.

CHAPTER 11
ALICE

I'm still trying to process my phone call with my mom—process what has become of my life—while lying on my bed like a dead fish, when my alarm goes off—a loud reminder that I need to get my shit together and get ready for work. *Happy birthday to me!*

I groan and roll onto my back, staring up at the stucco ceiling. My brain does not feel consistent. It feels like it's been put through a wood chipper and reassembled by a committee that can't agree on how many pieces there should be.

I'm not sure if I'm ready to deal with everything going on in my living room right now. I try, for maybe ten minutes, to pretend I'm still in control of my life, then finally get up.

I walk out of my bedroom, ready to get to work, only to walk into a brick wall of nakedness. I jump, startled.

Gage cocks his head. "Did you resolve your emotional conflict?"

"Working on it," I say. "So, are you going to measure everything in the bedroom now?"

He looks at me, genuinely confused by the idea that there's another option. "Yes," he says. "If you prefer I work somewhere else, please direct me."

There's a laugh in my throat that I can't swallow. "No, that is…fine.

I'm just trying to get used to..." I make a vague gesture trying to encompass all of him, which is a lot.

Gage senses my hesitation and steps closer, the tape measure retracting with a polite click. "Have I done something wrong?" The concern on his face is so devastatingly genuine that it breaks my heart.

I shake my head, averting my eyes. "God, no. I just...Can I get you something to wear? It's kind of hard to look at you with all that going on."

Gage considers, looks down at himself, and shrugs. "If it makes you more comfortable."

He surveys the room, then spots the laundry basket in the corner. He walks over, selects the most neutral pair of sweatpants (gray), and pulls them on with the ease of a mannequin at a department store. He asks, "Is this satisfactory?"

The waistband sits comically low—the pants are multiple sizes too small—but it's an improvement. He's still head-splitting hot.

I sigh and pinch the bridge of my nose, my head throbbing from the bottle of wine I drank and did not fuck. "Yes, thank you."

He waits patiently. When I don't speak, he offers, "Would you like me to prepare breakfast? I have learned several efficient methods for eggs. That, along with coffee, should relieve your hangover."

I blink. "You can cook?"

He nods, matter-of-fact. "It is a skill I have recently gained."

"That would be wonderful. Can you make omelets?"

"That is a method I have learned, yes."

I want to test his skills. I'm sure whatever he makes will be better than anything I can make. "Okay, cool."

He leaves the room smooth and quick and heads right for the kitchen. He announces, "I prepared your coffee for you," gesturing at the pot of brewed goodness. He measures creamer quickly and precisely, then pours it and coffee into my favorite cup. He removes something from the freezer, plops it into the concoction, then hands it to me.

I glare down, weary of what he put in my coffee, only to see a heart-shaped ice cube. "What's this?"

"I have calibrated the coffee to your exact specifications. The ice cube will bring the coffee to your preferred temperature more quickly, allowing for immediate consumption."

"Oh, wow. Thank you. This is...thoughtful," I say, sipping the perfectly "calibrated" coffee.

"You summoned me," he says. "I exist to serve your needs."

Gage returns to the fridge, measuring the door as he opens it, before retrieving ingredients I didn't realize were in there. Either they materialized with him—the "accessories" my dad mentioned—or they were in my fridge all along. I'm going to pretend the answer is "materialization," even though I know it's probably "it was behind your mess of old food, hidden from your too-impatient-to-look-thoroughly sight."

I watch him cook, marveling at the sexy, deliberate precision of his actions. First, he butters the pan with careful, even strokes. Then he cracks the eggs one-handed, as if he were some classically trained omelet chef, and sprinkles the cheese with the precision of someone who has never eyeballed the ingredients in a recipe before.

As he folds the egg in the pan, I wonder what transferable sex golem skill prepared him for this moment. I don't need to wonder too long because he caresses and spanks that thing with the spatula in a way that sends a wave of lustful heat through me.

While the omelet cooks, he slots slices of bread into the toaster, then taps them gently to ensure they stand perfectly parallel.

When the food is ready, he presents it to me, plated as if he were preparing a geometric work of art.

He stands behind the counter, watching for approval, eyes shining with devotion.

I take a bite. *Holy crap! It's the best omelet I've ever had.* I look up, mouth full, and say, "This is amazing!"

"Is there anything else I can do for you?"

I shake my head.

He beams, turns to measure the salt shaker, then hurriedly begins organizing my kitchen.

While eating the world's most symmetrical omelet, I turn, observing the rest of my unrecognizable apartment. I didn't even realize my apartment could be this clean. It turns out all my shit actually does have a proper place; I just haven't been using it. "Wow, Gage. You've been super busy."

"I have made several changes that should improve your quality of life. I hope you find them optimal."

"I do. Thank you."

He returns to his work, and I try to come to terms with the fact that my new housemate is a sentient object with a foot-long cock and an irresistible urge to optimize my life.

Mom said I should let him do all of this. That he essentially needs an outlet for his drive to please, but he is relentless—measuring, adjusting, jotting, reporting…annoying.

Eventually, I can't take it anymore.

I wipe my mouth and say, "Hey, Gage, can I talk to you for a second?"

He halts mid-action (measuring the depth of the sink) and turns as his tape measure slides closed, giving me his full attention. "Yes?"

There's something endearing about how fast he comes to stand in front of me, sweatpants riding low on his sharp hips, measuring tape coiled at his side like a gunslinger's holster. *Bright-blue-eyed and bushy-tailed.*

I gesture to the notebook. "Do you always have to do that? The… measuring?"

He looks down at the book, then at me, then back. "I'm a ruler."

I sigh, rake my fingers through my hair. "You're a human now."

He considers, frowns. "I am a human who measures."

I almost laugh. "Okay, sure. But, would you like to relax?"

He stares at me blankly. "If that is your preference."

I ask. "But what is your preference?"

"To meet your specifications."

I sigh, walk to the couch, and pat the seat next to me. "Sit."

He sits. Right next to me. Not in the way a normal person does, either—he sits with perfect posture, arms folded, hands resting on his knees, waiting for further instructions.

It's so awkward, so formal, that I burst out giggling.

He looks concerned. "Did I do it wrong?"

"No, you're fine. You're just…a lot."

He pauses, thinks hard. "A lot of what? What is the unit of measure?"

I roll my eyes, but can't help smiling. "Umm…I don't know. It's just a saying."

"Oh," he says, thumbing the spiral in his notebook.

I ask quietly, "Gage, why are you doing all this? Why are you measuring everything?"

He stops reviewing his notes, turns to me, and says, "This is what I do. I measure things with absolute precision. And I measure them for you."

There's a lump in my throat that I can't quite clear. "What if I just wanted you to…be with me? Not measure, not improve. Just exist."

He blinks, surprised. "If that is what you want, I will do it." He takes my hand, cradling it with both of his. "I want to be what you need."

I look at our joined hands, and something twists in my stomach.

Did I create him just to be my servant? This feels…wrong.

CHAPTER 12
GAGE

The couch feels too small for both of us, which doesn't make logical sense. There is 2.4 feet of empty space to her left and 3.5 inches between us.

Her hands are folded in her lap, fidgeting with the drawstring of her hoodie, winding and unwinding the cord, making and unmaking little nooses. She's staring at the television, which isn't even on. Her mind is turning something over, but I'm not sure what.

I want to ask what's wrong, but I know the answer: I am what's wrong.

Either I am wrong—incorrectly calibrated—or I did something wrong.

"Did I do something wrong?" I ask because in my extremely limited experience, wrongness can be corrected with enough information—*unless it's me that's wrong. I'm immutable now.*

She shakes her head, hair falling into her eyes. "No, it's not you. It's just—" She makes a gesture, as if stirring the air. "Everything is weird, okay?"

I nod.

It is weird.

I have only existed for seven hours and forty-five minutes. I have spent most of that time either inside her or optimizing the layout of her apartment.

This is not a rejection, but it has all the spectral properties of one. I want to apologize, but I don't know what for.

I run through the last ten minutes of our conversation, rewatching every facial tic, analyzing every syllable. She said I was "a lot," and then, "What if I just wanted you to…be with me? Not measure, not improve. Just exist."

What does it mean to 'just exist'?

I try to imagine it—being inert and pointless—but my mind slips off the edges.

I only know how to act. I only know how to serve.

I test the idea, and I arrange my limbs for optimal non-intrusiveness. My body fights the impulse to move, to help, to do. The silence is itchy and uncomfortable. I remain perfectly still for three full seconds, just existing.

But then, unable to resist the impulse, I run the tape measure out a little and watch the numbers flick by.

She glances sideways at me. "I just need to get my head together, okay?"

I don't understand what she means; the structure of her head seems fully assembled. I'm not sure how I could assist with this. "Perhaps I could measure its circumference for you," I say, certain I am missing something fundamental about her statement but determined to find out what it is.

She snorts, but it's not a laugh. "Gage, you don't have to measure everything. Or—" She pauses, searching for the correct phrase. "You don't have to do anything, actually. You can just sit."

Just sit. Okay. I can just sit.

I inch closer, reducing the gap to 1.7 inches, and try to just…sit.

I make it five seconds this time.

The impulse to move, to fix, to understand, overwhelms me. I reach for my spiral notebook and flip through the pages, finding my target.

MY LIFE'S PURPOSE (AN UNORDERED, ABRIDGED LIST):
1. **BE USEFUL**
2. **BE FUN**
3. **BE FUCKABLE (CRITICAL!!)**

I am not sure which of these will fix the current situation, but I start with the first one. "Would you like tea?" I ask, keeping my voice gentle.

She shakes her head, not even glancing up. "No, thanks. I'm good."

I scan her body for signs of dehydration or hunger, but there are none.

I try number two: "Want to play a game?" I ask, careful not to sound desperate.

She lets out a long sigh. "No. Gage. I'm serious. I just want to sit here for a while. In silence, okay?"

How long is 'a while'? Is fifteen seconds 'a while' because it feels like an eternity?

I wait sixteen seconds just to be sure, and then try number three. "Would you like to have intercourse?"

She laughs, but it's not a happy laugh. It's a little too loud, a little too sharp. "No, Gage."

The sentence lands on me like a sledgehammer. All motion ceases.

She closes her eyes, and for a moment her face crumples, then smoothes out. "I can't," she says, voice flat. "I have to work in a few minutes."

"I can bring you to orgasm in less than a few minutes, assuming a few is three."

"I said no," she says with a harsh finality.

Something wholly unfamiliar, since everything is unfamiliar, happens to my body. I didn't even know my face could do the thing it's doing, but I feel the muscles sag, the eyes droop, the corners of the mouth descend. My shoulders drop, measurable by a full four centimeters.

The space between us grows to 4.0 inches, then 4.3.

Her expression softens, as if she's aware of how abrupt she's being.

"I'm not mad, Gage, I'm just not feeling it," she says, and for some reason, that makes it worse.

I nod, even though my neck feels tight. "Of course. I will not initiate further."

She softens. "Hey. I mean it. You don't have to...perform all the time. You can just chill. You can sit with me. You don't have to serve me."

I sit. Not because I understand, but because the command is clear.

I think about the men who disappointed Alice, the ones who came up short. I am not sure how to avoid joining them.

Am I no longer desirable to her? Do my 12 inches no longer measure up?

"I apologize that I have not met your requirements," I say through a weird pain in my throat.

She leans back and closes her eyes. "Gage," she says. "I'm sorry. It's really not that. I am just thinking about something—" She trails off, and I sense she doesn't have the right tool for this problem either.

She stares at the ceiling for a while, silent. I match her, stare at the same spot. A crack runs from the light fixture to the corner of the room, zigzagging like a little river.

I want to fix it for her. I want to fix everything. I want to fix whatever is happening inside my ribcage.

She pulls her knees up and hugs them to her chest. The cute cat boxers ride up her thighs. I notice, but do not comment. She says, "You just...wouldn't get it, which isn't your fault. I guess."

I nod and clear my throat for the very first time, compelled for reasons I don't quite understand.

She's right. I wouldn't understand.

Alice opens her eyes and fixes them on me. She softens, rounding the sharp edges of her face. "Gage," she says, "I'm serious. You didn't do anything wrong. I promise."

But, for some reason, I don't believe her.

She looks at her phone and curses. "Shit." She places it face down on the coffee table and turns to me, grabbing both of my hands and turning my attention to her. "Gage. I'm sorry, but I have to go to work. Listen, I'll be right over there all day." She points to the corner of the dining room where her desk sits. "We can still hang out. I just have an important meeting today. Is that okay?"

Is it okay? Why would she ask me?

"If you say it is okay, then it is okay."

"No, I mean, will you be okay?"

Will I be okay? I don't know. Does she deem me sufficient?

I open my mouth to ask her if I have measured up sufficiently to be deemed "okay," but her face is twisted in worry, and I don't wish to twist it further. So, instead, I just nod, which I think is the reaction she is looking for.

"Okay," she says, and the worry smooths from her face.

She kisses me on the cheek and smiles at me. I return the smile even though my face doesn't want to.

She pushes herself up off the couch and walks over to her office area. The gap between Alice and me stretches, the distance increasing, and I don't know how to close it.

She sits, pulls her knees up under her, pulls the keyboard toward her, and begins to type with focused violence.

I sit where she left me, staring at the spot on the couch where the fibers are compressed by her absence. I am not sure if I am waiting for her to return, or for some new instruction, or just for the next opportunity to be useful.

What does she want me to be? I open the spiral notebook, flip to a blank page, and start a new list:

HOW TO BE USEFUL (WHEN NOT MEASURING OR FUCKING):

1. OBSERVE ALICE. (BUT NOT IN A CREEPY WAY.)

2. LEARN HER PREFERENCES, EVEN THE ONES SHE DOESN'T SAY OUT LOUD.

3. OFFER ASSISTANCE, BUT DON'T FORCE IT.

4. WAIT.

5. REPEAT AS NECESSARY.

I run through the list. None of it seems actionable.

For the next 37 minutes, I measure the distance between us. It never grows beyond 15 feet.

CHAPTER 13
GAGE

I lose track of time, which is the highest form of humiliation for an ex-ruler, thinking about what she said: "Not measure, not improve. Just exist," and, "just sit."

I try to do it. I sit, unmoving, for what feels like hours, but in reality, it's much less than that.

She clacks away at her keyboard, in a zone of non-distractibility, and doesn't look at me. She doesn't look anywhere but the screen. Her hands fly across the keys, pausing only to bring the coffee mug to her mouth.

Sitting here, unmoving, unacknowledged, makes me feel like I'm shoved in a drawer, forgotten…again.

After a while, she stands, stretches, and walks past me to the bathroom. She brushes her hand lightly over my shoulder as she goes, a gesture of acknowledgement that feels like what I've been waiting for.

But she disappears out of sight to the bathroom, and I feel like the light of my world has blinked out again.

Drawer closed. Darkness.

When she returns, she smiles at me, re-lighting my existence. She's removed her sweatshirt and now just wears a thin T-shirt. Her nipples print gentle ghosts through the thin fabric.

A tingling sensation rips through me, causing a pressure I can't quite categorize.

I watch her sashay to her chair. When she sits, she glances up, catches me watching, and gives a cute smile. She pulls her legs up to sit cross-legged on her chair, and her underwear peeks through her little cat shorts.

The tingling pressure warms and tightens.

She swivels her chair toward me. "You don't have to just sit there, you know. You can do whatever you want."

"So, you no longer wish for me to sit here?"

"I want you to do whatever you want to do, Gage."

Oh, okay.

I nod.

What do I want?

Last night, I made her laugh and come, both of which seem like top-tier accomplishments.

I'd like to do that again.

I want to make her come so badly that it literally hurts in my core—but she said she did not wish to have intercourse.

I look down and notice my cock is hard, which is strange because Alice and I are not currently copulating, and I am not actively performing.

A hot, plastic panic simmers in my chest.

I stand and pace, unsure why my body is behaving this way. I open my tape measure, run it over the length of the room, write the result in the notebook, then do it again just to see if maybe the world has shifted.

It hasn't.

I consider measuring my cock, but worry that doing so will cause it to malfunction further.

I look to Alice. She's hunched over her screen. Her hair has come loose from its bun, and a strand dangles in front of her face. She keeps blowing it away, but it always falls back. It's adorable.

My cock throbs.

She turns, sees me standing here, hovering, watching—probably being creepy, unable to follow my own rules.

"Hey, Gage," she says. "Did you have breakfast?"

I answer instantly: "I have no metabolic needs."

My stomach growls.

She laughs. "It kinda sounds like you do. You should eat something, Gage. You're human now. You need to eat."

Huh. Interesting.

I write this down in my notebook.

I go to the kitchen and open the fridge. I stare inside, memorize the contents, and close it.

What would I even eat?

I open the fridge again to see if the arrangement has changed.

It hasn't.

My reflection in the microwave catches my attention. I stare at my body. My face. My cock—still hard for no reason.

I measure my chest span, biceps, and even the distance between my nipples. I compare the results with what I recorded last night to see if they're different.

It isn't.

The sensation in my cock is different than last night: there's no obvious trigger, just a steady, ambient pressure. Once again, I consider measuring it to see if it has changed. But, I'm afraid it has changed. And afraid of what will happen to it if I touch it. Instead, I pull the waistband of the sweatpants tighter and retreat to the couch, hoping it will abate.

It doesn't.

I look to Alice again. Her legs are folded under her on the office chair, one bare foot dangling and flexing as she types. 90 degrees. 45 degrees. 90 degrees. 45 degrees. Every time she hits "Enter," she blows out a sharp exhale.

I want to be close to her, rub my erection against her thigh, and offer my services.

I watch her some more, and my arousal intensifies. There's no logic to it. She is not inviting me, not even making eye contact, but every nerve is singing. Every cell of my body wants to enter her.

Maybe this is the human experience? Spontaneous and unprovoked desire?

She rubs her neck, rolling her head, and I picture my hands doing that for her.

The urge becomes unbearable.

I know she said she didn't want to have intercourse, but…maybe she'll let me just touch her.

I put down the notebook, approach the desk, and kneel beside her chair. I wait for her to acknowledge me.

She does, in a voice that's more distracted than annoyed: "Gage, what's up?"

I try to explain the issue, but I can't make the words come out right. Instead, I rest my head against her thigh.

She stiffens, then relaxes, then runs a hand through my hair, absently. "You okay down there?"

I nod, but don't look up, appreciating the feel of her flesh against my cheek.

She looks down at me. "Gage, can you…give me, like, half an hour? I need to focus."

I nod, stand, and step back exactly three paces. I re-adjust the sweatpants, embarrassed by the visible tenting. "May I ask what one normally does when they have an erection and are not needed for sexual intercourse?"

Alice almost chokes on her coffee, then snorts. "Umm…you can take care of it yourself."

She looks at me like either a) she's horrified by my erection presenting itself in this moment when sexual gratification is not something she is requesting or b) the size of my idiocy surpasses the size of my erection, which we all know, is substantial.

It's probably b.

I just stand here, my fists clenched at my side, my dick hard as a rock, my eyes burning because they, too, are revolting against me.

She tilts her head, eyes narrowing. "Gage?"

"Yes, Alice?"

"Are you…okay?"

I consider the question. My body is malfunctioning. I don't know how to fix it, and even if I did, I don't know what I should be doing. She hasn't given me any directions. "I do not know what to do."

She returns her gaze to the computer monitor. "Try to relax. You should try eating something. "

I make a note of it. "I will do my best."

"Good." Her smile is soft and warm and makes my dick hard and hot.

I retreat to the far end of the couch, open the notebook, and try to log what just happened.

CHAPTER 14
ALICE

Gage is hovering. A lot. Currently, he thinks he's measuring the lintel of the kitchen, but really, he's measuring how long it takes before I lose my shit.

He watches me over the notebook, waiting, logging, never blinking, raging erection at my eye level.

I open the Slack channel for my team and try not to think about the urgent, pounding need in my pelvis that Gage spent all night fine-tuning: training my pussy to react with a Pavlovian pulse whenever his dick is in my vicinity.

I want to let him unleash all 12 inches of that glorious cock within me, fill the throb in the vacuum he left in my cunt, but I don't.

Instead, I let it metastasize into anxiety. Not only am I feeling epic levels of guilt over essentially bringing him into existence with the sole purpose of pleasing me, but I also have an important meeting at 10 am.

My team is pitching a new game concept to the CEO, and this morning they voluntold me to make the slide deck. "We just need a few slides," they said.

My life may be utter chaos, but my slide decks never are. I always put too much effort into them. Perfectionism runs through my veins. And right now, I'm so distracted by his dick that this deck is a disaster.

The meeting is fast approaching, and now I'm breaking into a cold sweat of imperfection. My mouse hand shakes, and I grip the side of my keyboard to steady it.

A shadow falls across one of my monitors. Gage has moved closer, a slow, measured step like he's in a wildlife documentary and I'm an easily-spooked prey animal. He doesn't speak, but he does that thing where he hovers just in my peripheral, a blue-eyed satellite always within range.

"Gage," I say, without looking up, "can you give me a minute?"

He hesitates, but then asks, "Sixty seconds?"

"I meant figuratively," I mutter, but he pulls the notebook to his chest and steps back, melting into the kitchen with the stealth of a highly-trained assassin.

I breathe. It doesn't help.

I get through three more slides, then the shadow returns, this time with a cup of coffee, already sweetened with the perfect amount of creamer. He sets it on the coaster with the precision of a bomb squad technician, then just stands there, waiting to be noticed.

I let him wait, because I don't want to yell at him for doing something nice but…I want to yell at him.

I don't look up until I've finished the line I'm writing, then glance at him. He's got the look of a child who's done something very clever and wants a gold star.

"Thank you," I say, not unkindly.

His face lights up. "Is there anything else I can do?"

"Not unless you can finish this presentation for me."

He processes for a second. "If you show me, I can."

I open my mouth to argue, but he's already circled behind me, peering over my shoulder at the laptop screen. I'm so used to being alone that the sensation of a man this close, so newly real and so intensely focused on me and so intensely sexy, sends a pulse of panic straight to my core.

He scans the slide for five seconds, then says, "You spelled 'initiative' wrong."

I glare at him. "Thank you, sentient spell check."

He takes a breath, like he's gathering his courage. "Would you like me to proofread? I can do it very quickly."

Something in me snaps. Maybe it's the lack of sleep, maybe the hangover from last night's orgy of emotional and literal penetration, maybe it's just the sight of his perfect, insufferable face so close to mine when I'm still not over the fact that my pussy is haunted by a magical Midas curse.

"Gage," I say, so abruptly even I flinch. I adjust my tone, trying for calm but landing somewhere between schoolmarm and total bitch, "I need you to stop hovering. Just—give me until after this meeting. Please."

He recoils, and the effect is so dramatic that for a second I think he might physically shrink. His shoulders hunch. He nods, notebook pressed tight to his chest, and takes three steps backward, the way an intern would if the CEO caught them stealing office supplies.

"I'm sorry," he says. "I thought you needed help."

I soften, but only a little. "You don't have to help all the time, okay? Sometimes I just want to be alone. It doesn't mean I'm mad at you."

He's quiet for a second, then says, "Are you sure?"

The question is so small and wounded that it punctures my balloon of rage.

I instantly regret everything. I've spent the last twenty-seven years being the only asshole in my own life, and now that there's another person in the apartment, I realize what it must be like to live with me.

"I'm sure," I say, softer. "I just need to prep for this meeting."

He stands there, waiting for approval, the way a cat does when it brings you the mangled corpse of a bird.

"Is there something else?" I ask.

He hesitates, then asks, "Do you still want me?"

The question hangs in the air, heavy and raw, and cracks my chest open.

I suddenly see last night from his point of view: summoned into existence, expected to be perfect, then told to go sit in the corner and not bother anyone.

No wonder he's weird. No wonder he's desperate to please. Mom warned me about this.

"Of course I do," I say, and to my own surprise, I mean it.

His face relaxes. "Okay."

He turns to go, but I stop him. "Wait, Gage?"

He pivots, hopeful.

"I'm sorry I was short with you," I say.

He shakes his head. "If you are not satisfied, then—"

"Gage," I cut him off, "it's not about satisfaction. It's about... boundaries. I just need space sometimes. It doesn't mean I don't like you."

He blinks, then nods, eyes dropping to the floor. "I will respect your boundaries. Thank you for the feedback."

He's so sincere it kills me.

He shuffles away and I stare at the slide deck.

I can't focus. My hands are shaking, but now it's not anxiety—it's guilt.

I take a deep breath, open Slack, and tap out: "Hey, everyone, not feeling great, and I need to take the rest of the day. The deck is done, just needs some proofreading. Good luck on the pitch!"

An immediate flurry of emojis and responses follow indicating my team will be more than fine without me.

CHAPTER 15
ALICE

Gage stands over the junk drawer, hands on either side of the laminate, not moving, just breathing slow and shallow.

"Gage?" I ask. "Do you want a hug?"

He stares at me, the confusion stopping all movements in their tracks. "Do you want to give me one?"

I swallow. "Yes," I say, "But do you want one, Gage?"

He blinks, runs a hand through his perfect hair. "Do I?" he asks, and it takes me a beat to realize he's not deflecting—he's genuinely asking.

"Yeah," I say. "I think you do."

We move toward each other like two people who are trying out a new dance for the first time. I open my arms first, and Gage steps into them, stiff and uncertain, then folds himself around me with a cautious kind of desperation. He's solid—maybe more solid than any man I've ever hugged—and large. But something about him feels small and fragile in this moment.

He rests his face against my neck and exhales.

"Sorry," I say into his hair, which smells like nothing, or maybe like the idea of hair. "I was an asshole earlier."

He's silent; he just holds on a little tighter.

"I'm serious," I say. "I snapped at you. I should have considered that maybe you're just as freaked out as I am by all this."

He pulls back, enough to look at me, but doesn't let go. "I am not freaked out."

I almost laugh. "You're not? Not even a little bit?"

He shakes his head, but then realization dawns on him. "Oh. Is that what is happening to me? Am I…freaking out?"

"I think so. What were you thinking about when you were looking in the drawer?"

He scrunches his face in a way you'd never expect someone so beautiful to do. "That I am not measuring up as a human. I don't understand this body or what I should be doing. And, my chest hurts."

"Your chest hurts?"

He nods, as if this is revelatory. "Yes, when I think about you being angry at me, my chest hurts."

I flinch. "I'm not angry. I'm…" I want to say "guilty," but that feels unfair to say.

"But…I thought you were angry and did not want me," he says, and his deep voice sounds so meek in this moment.

"Fuck," I say. "No, that's not it." I want to explain, but I don't even know where to start with this misunderstanding. "I'm sorry I gave you that impression."

"You do want me?" he asks, but there's a tremor in it.

"I do," I admit. "But I also feel shitty for…for making you like this. For bringing you into my mess of a life and making you responsible for my happiness, like you don't get a say."

He pulls back, but doesn't let go. "You feel bad for making me," he says.

I nod. "Yeah. It's not fair. You didn't ask to be here."

Gage looks at his hands, as if seeing them for the first time. "I didn't. But I'm glad I am." He looks up, and the blue in his eyes is bright in the kitchen light. "It's better than not existing."

I want to say something comforting, but I don't know how to make sense of his worldview. Instead, I reach out and run my thumb over the back of his hand.

"Sorry," I say again, but it comes out thin and useless.

He leans in, puts his head on my shoulder, and for a long minute, we just stand there.

My neck is suddenly wet.

Gage is crying. Not sobbing—just leaking, a slow and steady drip, like someone left a faucet on just a hair. His shoulders shake, but only slightly.

I put my arms around him, and the urge to fix his pain almost makes me dizzy.

He laughs, but it's a sad, busted sound. "What is happening to my face?"

"Tears," I say. "You're crying."

He pulls back, studies me, then wipes his cheek with the back of his hand. "Why?"

I search for an answer, but my throat is closing up. "Sometimes," I say, "when people have too many feelings, the feelings come out of their eyes."

He stares at me, uncomprehending. "Is it normal?"

I nod. "Yeah. It means you're human."

He thinks about this for a long time, then leans in and rests his forehead against mine. "Thank you for making me human, Alice."

And now I'm crying too, but I hide it by squeezing him so hard he squeaks.

CHAPTER 16
ALICE

I ask, "Are you okay?"

He nods, but his eyes are bright and red at the rims. "I don't like this feeling," he says, after a beat.

"Yeah, most people don't," I say. "I think it's, uh, a combo of lack of sleep, no food, and the whole existential crisis thing."

He blinks. "I don't need sleep. Or food."

I step out of his arms, but only to lean against the counter. "Gage, you're a human now. You need sleep and food."

He yawns at the exact moment his stomach growls.

He shakes his head, almost offended. "My body doesn't require energy, so fuel in the form of food and energy restoration in the form of sleep is wholly unnecessary."

I gesture broadly at him. "I hate to break it to you, but your body does require energy. Listen, I just found out my dad used to be a calculator watch, but he most definitely has to eat and sleep. I've seen him pass out after Thanksgiving dinner enough times to know it's true."

He's silent for a while. Then: "What would I eat?"

I grin. "Literally anything."

He hesitates. "What if I don't like it?"

"You probably will," I say. "But if not, then you just eat something else. It's fun to experiment—calibrate your taste buds or whatever."

He runs a thumb over his bottom lip, as if tasting the idea. "Do you think it will help?"

I shrug. "Couldn't hurt. Here, sit." I pat the kitchen stool and grab the bread. "We're going to start with something kind of basic. Toast." *Finally, someone I can cook for with my skill level.*

He sits, spine straight, hands folded like he's about to take a test. I toast a slice and slather it with butter. I hand it over, and Gage inspects it like an artifact.

"Is this…good?" he asks.

"It's toast," I say, "it's the baseline. If you like this, we'll try something fancier like toast with strawberry preserves." I laugh.

He bites with the audible crunch of a man whom I'm going to have to teach table manners because no one else has. He chews, eyes going wide, and for a second, I worry he'll just swallow the whole thing, but he actually savors it. A tear glistens in his eye as he processes the flavor.

"It's warm," he says. "What is this flavor?"

I have to think about it for a while because I have no idea how to fucking describe basic-ass buttered toast. "I think it'd be considered savory. And a little salty."

He takes another bite, and another. By the time he finishes, he looks better. Not fixed, but less like he is contemplating shoving his whole body into the junk drawer.

"I still don't want to sleep," he says.

"You will," I promise. "You'll probably do it without trying. Or you'll get so tired you hallucinate. I don't recommend waiting that long."

He laughs, wipes his mouth with the back of his hand. "Do I have to do this every day?"

"Multiple times a day."

He's quiet, thinking. "What else do I need to start doing?"

Well, now you're going to have to use the bathroom in a few hours, but I don't want to explain that to you just yet.

I lean on the counter, cross my arms. "A lot. Luckily, you already know how to do all the hard stuff like walk and read." I laugh. "But, I guess you gotta learn all the basics of having a body."

He looks at me, uncertainty and hope fighting across his face. "Were you always this good at existing?"

I snort. "Absolutely not. I was lucky enough to have a baby phase. That's when most humans get a free pass to learn and kind of fuck stuff up."

"So, humans use their baby phase to figure out what to do with themselves?"

I laugh, a hard single exhale. "No. We spend our whole lives trying to figure that out. But, we do figure out how to do our basic functions after the baby phase, at least."

He tilts his head, storing that fact. "I will try to be as good at living as you are."

I give him a side-eye. "Set the bar a little higher, Gage."

He smiles, and it's the first time I've seen it without any trace of sadness. "I will do my best, but you are the bar," he says. "You will always be the metric against which everything is measured."

I want to hug him again, but I settle for getting him a glass of water. "You also have to drink water. Lots of it. Definitely don't decide how much by watching me because I don't drink nearly enough, and you need more since you're bigger."

He sips it. "My tongue is broken! It has no taste, only wetness."

I laugh. "Water doesn't usually have a taste. It is like the baseline for all drinks."

He writes something down, and I pour him a cup of black coffee, no creamer. "Okay, we're swinging pretty far from baseline with this one. What do you think?"

"I don't like it," he says, but continues to drink it, anyway.

* * *

I lean across the counter, watching Gage demolish a second piece of toast, this time with more confidence and with strawberry preserves, and fewer existential tears.

"So, I took the day off work to hang out with you," I say.

He finishes chewing, then looks at me, face suddenly serious. "Why?"

I laugh, rubbing a crust from the corner of his mouth with my thumb. "Because it's our birthday."

He looks at the clock. "It's my birthday? I thought it was your birthday."

"Yeah. You were created after midnight, which means it is your birthday, too. Happy birthday, Gage."

He smiles a small smile, then looks down at his spiral notebook, flips to a clean page, and writes in big block letters: "TODAY IS OUR BIRTHDAY."

CHAPTER 17
GAGE

I stare at the last crumb of toast on the plate, trying to decide if I am supposed to want it, or if wanting is the entire point. My hands still tremble—but less so, and I think Alice was correct about my body needing energy.

I write in my notebook:

HUNGER = TREMBLING HANDS?

Alice leans across the counter, watching me not eat, her chin propped on her palm. "I'm glad you like toast," she says, voice low and shy. "It's…pretty much the only thing I can make."

Her hair falls into her face, and she smiles a half-smile at me.

That tingling feeling in my gut I now recognize as unprompted arousal returns, but this time it's not as frightening—it's actually kind of pleasant.

"I like toast," I say to confirm. "Very much. I think I like you more, though." This is true, but also not what I meant to say; it came out unprompted.

She flushes, looking away, but the smile that splits her face intensifies my erection. "Well, good. Because you're stuck with me, birthday boy."

She says "birthday boy" in a way that I interpret as erotic and elicit, and I do think she did that on purpose.

Alice gets up and rounds the island, slumping into the stool next to mine. She smells like strawberry preserves and a little like sweat, and I want to lick both off her. She leans in, shoulder to shoulder, and says, "So what do you want to do for your first birthday?"

I blink. "I did not consider the possibility of celebration."

She grins, nudges my thigh with hers. "C'mon, Gage. You're a real boy now. What do you want to do?"

I think. Hard. It's the sort of question you don't want to answer wrong, especially when the person asking is the entire reason for your existence.

I run through a list of possibilities: *Sex (obvious—well, it is now, anyway), measuring things (already did that), making more toast (appealing, but repetitive).*

I dig deeper, looking for a true wish. Something monumental.

"Can I…" I hesitate, because what I want seems both small and huge. "Can I try things I've never tried before?"

Alice laughs. It's a real laugh, short and barky. "That's the whole point, silly. It's your birthday."

I process. "I would like to eat cake."

She claps as if that's exactly what she wanted as well. "Done. We'll go to the store and get you a cake. Any kind you want. Maybe even a candle. I guess technically you're zero, but we can call this one."

She bounces on her heels, and the way her braless breasts bounce makes me think that discounting sex was a bad idea. Cake sounds amazing. But I can eat cake afterwards.

I can have my cake and fuck her, too.

I want to kiss her, but I am distracted by the next wave of physiological needs.

My mouth stretches into a yawn—a massive, jaw-aching one. I shudder, the muscles in my arms spasming.

Alice leans in and whispers, "You want me to teach you how to take care of that?" She glances meaningfully at my lap.

I am too embarrassed to answer, but she seems to get the message.

I yawn again, longer this time. My entire body feels heavy, dense, like I am being magnetized to the floor.

My erection is still there, stubborn and distracting.

She stands, ruffles my hair, and says, "Finish your coffee. I'm going to show you how to take care of both that erection and the yawn."

I drain it quickly, growing accustomed to the taste. When I'm finished, she tugs me up from the stool. "C'mon, let's take care of this before you break something."

I follow, only a little ashamed of how much I want her to take care of it.

Alice leads me to the bedroom, still holding my hand, and sits on the bed. She pats the comforter beside her for me to sit.

I perch on the edge, legs splayed to relieve the pressure in my groin. "What do I do?"

She takes a minute, as if she, too, doesn't know the directions. "Okay, so here's the thing. If you want me to, I can help. But it's also good to learn how to take care of it yourself."

The implication hits me all at once. Some knowledge I didn't realize I had: "Oh, masturbation."

She nods, attempting solemn, while repressing a grin. "Yep."

I feel my face heat, even as my cock gets harder under the fabric. *How much blood does this body have that it can rush to both places?*

I ask, "Do I just…do it now?"

She laughs, warm and bright. "You can, if you want. But you can also watch me, if that helps."

I'm so startled by the offer that I almost fall off the bed. "How would watching you help? Our anatomy is different."

She shrugs. "Some people like to have visual stimuli to go along with the physical."

I stare at her, waiting for her to rescind the offer, but she doesn't. Instead, she stands, pulls off her t-shirt, and tosses it aside.

Her breasts are small and high, the nipples are the most perfect pink. She touches one, rolling the nipple between thumb and finger. "Do you like watching me, Gage? If not, I can leave."

I do. "Stay," I nearly shout, afraid she'll leave. The pressure in my groin is so intense it feels like a new pulse.

"So, pull out your dick and show me how much you like watching me, Gage."

I reach under the waistband, curl my hand around my cock, and the sensation is electric.

I stroke, slow at first, then harder, matching the rhythm of Alice's breath as she plays with her nipples. She watches me, openly, biting her bottom lip.

The air is thick with the smell of sweat and arousal and her.

I jerk faster. Alice slips two fingers inside herself, while her first hand still pinches her nipple. She lets out a moan that short-circuits my brain.

This is chaos.

And it lasts exactly 2 minutes and 13 seconds.

When the orgasm hits, it's like being electrocuted. I come so hard I see blue, so bright I worry I've returned to my ruler state for a moment.

I arch back, toes curling, cock spurting white-hot. I am surprised my body can produce this stuff. Last night, when I came, I didn't get to see the result. But now, it arcs up, a line of white landing on my stomach.

And it doesn't stop. It's spurts and spurts and spurts, and just when I think my body is malfunctioning again, it stops, leaving me empty and shuddering.

She doesn't stop touching herself. In fact, she seems to like it—her breath stutters, and she lets out a low, guttural cry as she comes, too.

It took her exactly 3 minutes and 11 seconds.

This was most efficient of us.

I collapse back on the bed, panting, every muscle turned to jelly. "Thank you," I say, because it feels like the only thing I can say.

Alice pulls tissue from her nightstand—where I used to live—and reaches over to wipe the mess off my abs. "You're welcome, birthday boy."

For a moment, the whole world is reduced to the sight of her, sweat-soaked and grinning, cum glistening on her skin—I'm not even sure how it got on her, but it seems the stuff has a mind of its own.

I want to remember this forever.

She stretches, catlike, and pulls the comforter over me, grinning.

Another yawn rips through me, and my eyelid feels heavy. "That was…amazing."

I can feel her heartbeat against my side, thumping slow and even. I want to stay awake, to watch her breathe, but I can't.

My eyelids droop, heavy as lead. The last thing I hear is her voice, low and close and warm in my ear: "If you think that was amazing, wait till you try cake."

And then I am gone, floating in the dark, dreaming of cake and bodies and the wild, impossible fact of being alive.

Sleep swallows me whole.

CHAPTER 18
GAGE

There's a thump from the kitchen. Then another, heavier, followed by the slide-slap of plastic bags on the countertop.

She's back.

I roll out of bed and run my hand through my hair. It is standing up where my face was pressed against the pillow. My jaw is dotted with tiny, prickly stubble. *Does sleeping make this grow?*

I like it.

Maybe I'll grow a beard, since I guess that's something I can do.

I'll ask Alice if she'd like that.

I make myself presentable, I think, then follow the noise.

Alice stands at the kitchen island, arms buried to the elbows in plastic bags. She's changed her clothes, now wearing that hoodie again and some pants.

Disappointment that her nipples and legs are now chastely covered makes me wish she would give her clothing sentience, just so I could fight it.

She looks up, sees me, and grins. "Did I wake you? I'm sorry. How was your first nap?"

I'm too shy to say what I really want to say, which is: "I missed you.

Can you please put the shorts back on?" So, I say, "I think it was good."

I help her put the bags on the counter and ask, "What's all this?"

She unloads boxes onto the counter with the flourish of a saleswoman. "Every flavor of cake mix they had. Every frosting, too."

"Fourteen cake mixes," I say, "and twelve frostings? That is 168 cake and frosting combinations."

Alice nods. "I figured we could make a bunch of cupcakes. See which combos are best." She pauses, uncertainty flickering in her eyes. "Unless that's lame? You just seemed really into the cake idea."

I blink, taken aback by the effort and the expense. "That's not lame. That's—" I can't find a word that matches the warmth in my chest. "It's optimal."

She laughs, and it's music. "You're such a fucking dork, Gage." But she says it like it's the highest compliment.

I sidle up next to her, picking up a box at random. "Triple Chocolate Death. Is it possible to die from chocolate?"

"You are so literal," she laughs.

"It is my nature," I say, with a shrug.

She giggles again. "It's funny. You remind me a lot of my dad. Which…makes a lot of sense considering y'all's shared backgrounds." She grabs the box out of my hand and kisses me on the cheek. "Anyway, the pedantic answer, which I'm guessing you're looking for, is, 'if you're allergic or…maybe if you eat too much.' But the name is mostly hyperbolic—because it's fun. And chocolate is fun."

Death is fun? Well, this conversation is bringing me joy, so I guess maybe it is.

I attempt to line the boxes up by color, but Alice swats me away, saying, "No, no, no. We gotta sort them by deliciousness."

"I don't know how delicious they are."

"That's why you've got me, babe." I watch Alice move, her motions fluid and sure, even as she drops a can of strawberry frosting and curses under her breath. She's so alive it hurts. "I'm going to rank them, and you gotta tell me if my ranking is correct."

I touch her arm, just above the elbow. "It will not be your ranking that is incorrect, but mine."

She looks down at my hand, then up at my face. "I dunno...something tells me we might disagree on red velvet." She smirks, as she places the red velvet box at the end of the row.

"Then I guess we will see," I say with a smile, enjoying this game that I recognize is food-themed flirting.

She bends over, rummaging through a cabinet, and I forget about the cake for a moment. My dick is hard again, and I wonder if this insatiability is due to her hotness or my dick's newness.

She pops upward, placing multiple cupcake pans on the counter, and says, "So, I had this big plan to make a dozen cupcakes of each mix. So you could try every frosting on every cake flavor, if you wanted. But..."

"What?"

"Now, I think maybe I was overzealous. I'm a terrible cook. Like, legitimately bad. I almost burned the house down once, making pizza bagels in the microwave." She looks both proud and embarrassed, and it is the most adorable thing I've ever seen.

"Baking is just measuring and following rules," I say. "I could help. I'm very good at measuring and following rules."

She grins, biting the edge of her thumb. "Yeah, it's kind of your whole thing."

I want to kiss her right then, but she's already busy getting the other ingredients we will need.

"Do you want to start from the top or the bottom? Worst flavor first or best first?"

"What do you think?"

"I think I want to do what you want to do."

"Worst."

"Then we'll start with red velvet!"

* * *

The red velvet, pineapple, lemon, and Funfetti cupcakes have finished. The smell of baking sugar fills the apartment, sweet and heady.

"I've got a secret, I haven't ever had pineapple cake before. I ranked that one on vibes," Alice says, turning off the timer.

Alice puts on oven mitts and opens the oven door. "Wow, they smell good, though, huh?"

When she bends over, I enjoy the way her ass looks—my eyes water with pure happiness and the heat from the stove.

"Are you excited for frosting?" she asks.

"I am excited for everything," I say, and it's the truest thing I know. "Thank you for making me human."

CHAPTER 19
ALICE

The sugar crash hits us like a tranquilizer dart. I always thought they were made up. Something dentists tell children to save their teeth. I was wrong, which I am often, so it's not that big a deal. I sprawl on the couch, cupcake wrapper pressed to my face, and groan. "Oh, my God. I can't eat another bite."

Gage is beside me, legs stretched out, fingers laced over his stomach. His chest rises and falls like he's meditating. He looks so content, I'm half convinced he's going to fall asleep again.

I close my eyes, ready to pass out, as well.

"Are you in pain?" he asks.

"Yes. I might die." I don't open my eyes, but I know what his face must be doing. I clarify, "I'm being hyperbolic. I won't die."

He chuckles. "That's because you haven't eaten Triple Chocolate Death yet. That will surely kill you."

I open one eye to peer at him.

He's grinning at me, wide and unrepentant, proud of his joke.

I laugh at him, his joy infectious.

"I think it's time for me to take a nap now," I say, yawning. "Anything else you want to do for your birthday?"

Gage props himself on one elbow, leans in close, and says, "I'd rather not nap."

"Oh?" I play dumb, but my heart is already running the numbers.

His hand finds my knee, and his thumb traces a slow, absent circle. "Well, there is something I've wanted to do all day," he says.

His hand slides up my thigh, pausing for consent. I laugh, then cover his hand with mine. "Gage, are you saying you want birthday sex?"

He nods, back to his serious face. "Yes. If you do."

I roll my eyes, but there's no way to hide the smile. "You are insatiable."

He shrugs, unashamed. "You made me that way."

I burst out laughing. For a moment, we're just grinning idiots, staring at each other in a sugary haze.

"So, do you want to nap or…?" he asks, low.

I consider, then say, "Well, if I'm being honest. It was really hard watching you walk around all day in those slutty sweatpants rocking that foot-long boner all day."

He bites his lip, then sits up, pulls me into his lap with one smooth motion. I yelp, but it's a fake protest.

He tucks a strand of hair behind my ear. "Is that yes to intercourse?" he asks.

I nod. "Yes."

He kisses me then, deep and slow, and the taste of a million frostings is still on his tongue.

When the kiss breaks, he says, "I want to taste you again."

The words hit me somewhere low and delicious, and all I can do is nod.

He flips me so I'm sitting on the couch and looks at me with those impossibly blue eyes and says, "May I?" already lowering himself to kneel in front of me.

I lift my legs, digging my heels into the plush seating, and I spread my knees. "Be my guest."

Gage grins, hungry and reverent, as his eyes scan every square inch of my body.

He kisses my knee, just below the hem of the shorts he begged me to put back on earlier. He works a slow devotional path along my thigh.

He's just begun, and already my brain is a whirring, gelatinous mess.

He hooks his thumbs into the waistband of my shorts and underwear and pulls them both down slowly. His eyes are on my face the whole time.

When the fabric hits the floor, I'm exposed, bare to the waist and goosebumped from the chill and the insane, thrilling embarrassment of it all.

He kneels in front of me, hands on my knees, gently urging my legs apart. I open for him.

He doesn't go straight for the main event. He resumes his work on the insides of my thighs, kissing and licking until I'm shifting, trying to put his mouth on me.

When he finally does, it's not subtle. He licks from bottom to top, slow and steady, and then pauses, as if analyzing the aftertaste. "You're sweeter than frosting," he murmurs.

I snort, and the sudden release of tension makes me laugh, breathless. "You are such a dork."

He grins, then dives in. The first pass is gentle, exploratory. He teases, he samples, he finds the spot that makes my toes curl and then circles back to it, again and again.

He's not methodical—he's obsessed. If there's ever been a man more invested in the outcome of eating pussy, I haven't met him.

His tongue is strong and precise—the stubble on his jaw scratches in a way that is surprising and pleasant.

Every flick, every pause, every inhale is tuned to my response.

If I twitch, he doubles down; if I moan, he slows, as if to make the sensation last.

I lean back, elbows locked, and tilt my head to the ceiling, trying to catalog the feeling. There's too much to hold at once: the plush couch under my ass, the heat of his mouth, the reverent hum he makes when he's really, really into it.

He pushes two fingers inside me, slow and careful, and my hips jerk like he's hit a live wire.

"Sorry," he says, mouth muffled against my skin. "Was that okay?"

I grab his hair and pull him back in. "Better than okay."

He works me with his hand and mouth at the same time, and I can hear the wet, obscene sounds—no table manners.

I want to be embarrassed, but I'm not.

I want to be quiet, but I can't, because I have no table manners either.

He keeps going, licking and sucking, relentless, until the pressure builds so tight I can't see straight. I bite my knuckle to keep from screaming, but then I remember there's no one here but us, and I let go.

The orgasm hits harder than I expect, sharp and sudden.

My whole body shudders. He holds my thighs apart and doesn't let up, drawing it out until I'm gasping, tears running down the sides of my face.

CHAPTER 20
GAGE

I'm still on my knees when the aftershocks ripple through her. Alice's thighs tremble around my ears, squeezing, then releasing, then squeezing again with an involuntary twitch. She tastes like salt and sugar and—unexpectedly—lemon frosting, but that's probably the cupcake I ate before I ate her.

My tongue flicks her clit one last time, and she yelps, then goes limp, which, as someone who spent his entire pre-life-life as a mostly inflexible stick of plastic, I find quite endearing.

I lean back on my heels, grinning and proud, and watch her descend from orbit.

She's so beautiful.

She opens her eyes and blinks at the ceiling, then at me, giving me a dazed little smile. "Holy shit," she says. "You're…good at that."

I beam and say, "It's what I was made for."

She laughs so hard she almost falls off the couch. "I suppose so."

She's naked from the waist down except for a single sock with cupcake frosting on it. I don't know what happened to the other sock. It's likely lost to the void that objects, especially socks, get lost in. I'd be sad for it, if I weren't so happy.

I pat her hip and try not to look too pleased with myself, as I hug her to my chest.

She recovers fast, and I wonder if the fact that she's technically the descendant of countless "sex golems" means she's essentially built for fucking like I am.

She straightens up with a grin. "Alright, birthday boy. It's your turn."

I try to process what she's saying, but my brain is still in devour mode. "My turn for what?"

She stands and wobbles slightly, bouncing with an adorable combination of excitement and jelly legs.

She points where she stood, and commands, "Sit," pushing me gently.

I sit, because the one thing stronger than my need to please is gravity.

She hovers over me, grinning with mischievousness, tilts her head, and says, "I know one other thing you've never experienced."

"The list is uncountable. I will need more of a hint."

"A blowjob," she says, placing her hands on her hips like some pantless blowjob-giving superhero.

She's right. She always is. I have never had one, and until this moment, I didn't know I wanted one, but now the thought of receiving one consumes my mind like a wildfire.

She grins, delighted, and reaches for the waistband of my sweats, tugging, slow and deliberate. "Would you like one?" she asks.

I nod, throat dry.

She slides my pants down, and my cock bobs out, already hard. She eyes it, then looks up at me, blue-green irises almost mocking. "Consider this a birthday present."

I want to say something, but the only sound I make is a whimper.

She leans in front of me and wraps her hand around the shaft, thumb circling the head. The touch is electric, ten times more intense than when I did it myself earlier today.

She strokes, slow at first, then with more confidence, and the whole world narrows to the friction of her palm and the heat of her skin.

"God," she murmurs. "Your dick is huge."

I open my mouth to say something about how she designed me that way or that I'm "to spec," but instead I just say, "Uuuuuuuh."

She sinks to her knees on the rug in front of me, licking her lips and making the same face she did right before she ate her favorite cupcake and frosting combination.

She cups my balls with one hand and traces her tongue up the underside of my dick, slow and deliberate.

I nearly come right then. I clamp my hands to my thighs, white-knuckled.

She notices and grins up at me. "You like that?"

"Very much," I manage.

She laughs. Then she returns her mouth to me, tightening her lips around the head and swirling her tongue. It's hot, slick, impossibly soft, with a ghosting hint of teeth that makes the act seem dangerous, and even more arousing.

Then there's a pressure and a pull as she hollows out her cheeks at the exact moment she bobs downward, and the world fractures into nothing but numbers and the sensation around my cock.

She bobs up and down, slowly, taking me deeper each time she descends, each fraction of an inch ticking off in my mind, as she descends and ascends.

My vision blurs. My toes curl.

And when my head touches the back of her throat, it feels like a measuring tape materializes into my chest, fully extended, then snaps back, quick and violent and loud. I moan so loud the sound vibrates through me and into her throat, as if the voice came from us both.

She lets my dick pop out of her mouth with a wet, obscene sound, and the air feels cold against my wet cock, making me miss the heat of her, but also somehow turning me on even more.

She locks eyes with me, with a wicked grin. "How does that feel?"

I can't speak.

I just nod, mouth open, eyes wide, whimpering.

She wipes her mouth with the back of her hand, then dives back in, deeper this time. And then, she hums, vibrating her throat, my cock, and somehow my left leg, which now twitches at my side: another malfunction, but I couldn't give less of a fuck right now.

She uses both hands, twisting, squeezing, coordinating with her mouth in a way that makes my brain stop working.

Now that I'm mortal, I can die. And I think this might be the thing that does me in. And I'm okay with that.

Here lies Gage, who didn't even make it twenty-four hours. Done in by a blowjob. Lived the best fucking life ever—literally and figuratively; he spent most of it fucking.

My abs tighten and my ass clenches. I lift off the couch a little, thrusting into her just slightly, but not enough to change her pace because she's relentless.

Maybe one of her grandfathers was a vacuum. Thank Dionysus for that.

Her pace builds, faster, wetter, her tongue doing things I didn't know were possible.

She glances up, makes eye contact, and the look in her eyes—hungry, proud, and daring—pushes me over the edge.

I come with a force that blanks out my vision.

My hips buck as the entire life force she gave me drains from my body and shoots into the back of her mouth.

It's dizzying.

She milks the last spasms out, then lets my dick fall onto my stomach, twitching and leaking.

She swallows everything, not missing a drop, and I wonder what it tastes like. *Does she like my taste as much as I like hers?*

For a moment, I am floating, weightless and numb.

Alice crawls up next to me on the couch and wipes her chin. She leans over, plants a kiss on my forehead, and whispers, "Happy birthday, Gage."

I smile, dazed, and pull her into my lap. "Happy birthday, Alice."

We stay there, sticky and exhausted, for a long time.

She strokes my hair, and I run my fingers up her back, feeling the shiver each time I touch the base of her neck.

Finally, she pulls back and says, "So, what did you think?"

I shake my head, still reeling. "I finally understand the phrase 'mind blown.'"

She laughs, bright and sharp. "You're adorable."

CHAPTER 21
GAGE

"Alice," I say, voice hoarse. I think maybe I have a soul now, and I think it's vibrating—cocooned in the bliss of the moment.

Her head is on my chest, and my arms are wrapped around her tight enough to fuse us at the ribs. She stretches, arching against me, and mumbles, "Yeah, Gage?"

"I love you." I didn't even really know what love was before today, but I know I love her. I know it with unerring certainty. I know it to be truer than anything I've ever known.

She sits up, bracing her hands on my chest, and studies my face. "You love me?"

"Yeah," I say, because there's no point hiding it. "I think I did before you even made me human. I think I have since I sat in your third-grade pencil cup."

She bites her lower lip, then smiles, tears glimmering in her lashes. "You remember that?"

"Yeah."

She shakes her head, a tiny, private laugh bubbling up. "I think I love you, too." She looks almost surprised by the admission, like it snuck up on her from behind a bookcase. "I know I just met you, but it feels like I've known you my whole life."

I pull her close, pressing my forehead to hers. "Well, you've definitely known me my whole life."

She laughs, and I think I'm starting to get the hang of how to do it: make her laugh.

I don't measure the time we spend here together, embracing. I don't measure anything. I just breathe her in. I just…exist.

Oh, I get it…this is nice.

And then my cock, wants to join in on the conversation. The initial nudge is subtle, as if it's tapping me on the thigh, saying, "Hey, Gage, whatcha talking about?" But within seconds, it's at full mast, standing, yelling, "Hey, dickhead. Include me in the conversation!"

Alice pulls back, gaping. "You're—" She gestures at my leaking, insistent dick. "You just came, like, two minutes ago."

"Sorry," I say, but it's not really an apology.

She slides her hand down and wraps it around my shaft, eyes wide in admiration. "How are you hard already?"

And now I kind of wish I had measured the time, because I'd like to write down how long my refractory period lasts in my notebook.

I consider, then admit, "As I mentioned, I was technically made for this function—sex golem, remember."

She laughs, then shakes her head, climbing onto my lap, straddling me, and for a moment it's just kissing—long, greedy, full-body kisses that steal my breath and make my dick bounce, happy to be included in the conversation finally.

Her hands run up and down my torso, still learning the map of my body.

I dig my fingers into her hips. "I would like intercourse as my next birthday present."

She smirks, hips grinding against me. "Good thing we consumed all those cupcake calories, because I'm going to need a lot of energy to keep up with you."

I guide her hips, aligning myself, and she sinks onto me in one slow, shuddering motion.

The feeling is even better than last night: hotter, wetter, and so tight I think I might black out.

She rocks back and forth, rhythm picking up speed, hands braced on my shoulders.

Every time she drops down, the world narrows to that single point of contact. I lift her shirt to her throat. Her tits bounce, and I can't stop staring—every detail, every movement, burned into my memory.

"Oh, fuck," she gasps. "You're so fucking big."

I beam, then pull her down for a kiss. "Built to spec."

She rides me hard, sweat slicking our bodies, her nails digging crescents into my back. I thrust up to meet her, and she yelps, startled at the force. "Oh, Gage—"

And I want to hear her scream my name over and over.

I wrap my arms around her, squeezing tight, and angle my hips just so.

She cries out, "Yes, Gage," and I think I've found the exact spot that I need to poke to get her to say my name. I'll write it down the first moment I get.

She clamps down, pussy spasming around me, and I know she's close.

I reach between us and rub her clit, using the knowledge built into my DNA, which I assume I have now.

She screams and starts to convulse.

Watching her come is the best thing I've ever seen. I never want it to end, but when it does, I'm ready to make her do it again.

I slide out from underneath her and turn her so she kneels on the couch facing its back.

I lift her ass, guide her hips, and align myself.

I watch, wide-eyed, as my dick slowly sinks into her beautiful folds.

She's resting her head on the couch, blissed out, but when I sink fully to the hilt, reaching a spot I am certain no one else ever has, she wails even louder than before.

"That's my spot," I growl, as if I were an explorer, planting my flag in uncharted territory.

The first time I entered her, there was pleasure, sure, but my mind was so focused on pleasing her, I didn't let myself fully enjoy it—it was not my purpose to come, after all.

But now, as I bask in the beauty of her, bask in my love for her, I can't help but let myself feel everything. And everything is fantastic and overwhelming.

I grab her hips and slam into her, hard and fast, and set a brutalizing pace. I suspect her to protest, but instead she just slams back into me, as if to say, "Is that all you got?"

So I give her more.

I reach around and press my fingers firmly on her clit, circling hard, determined to make her come again.

For a moment, I think I might fail at my mission, because a heat builds, starting at the base of my spine, and I worry that maybe eating cupcakes has made me less effective at my primary function.

But she shutters, and clenches, and wails my name, biting the back of the couch just in time to come as the heat within me explodes outward.

Jet after jet of hot, thick cum pulses so deep inside her that I think, maybe, I am fully spent.

We collapse onto the couch, bodies a tangle of limbs and sweat and post-coital euphoria.

She nestles into my chest, hair damp and wild, and traces lazy circles over my abs. "I can't believe I get to keep you," she whispers.

I kiss the top of her head. "You're the only reason I exist."

She looks up, eyes glossy but fierce. "Does that make me a selfish person? Creating you and then…I dunno, just using you for sex?"

I grin, nuzzling her ear. "I don't think so. I feel like that time I was using you for sex."

She laughs, pure and unguarded, and the sound is so perfect I want to catch it and pin it on a board to display like a butterfly.

She dozes, cheek pressed to my chest, and I watch her breathe, counting each rise—back to measuring, unable to stop myself.

Thank you, Dionysus. Thank you for giving her, and in turn me, this gift.

CHAPTER 22
ALICE

I'm not sure what the average duration is for a post-cupcake fuck marathon, but I suspect we're in the upper 0.5% percentile and still climbing.

Time has turned to molasses, sticky and slow.

I'm not ashamed to admit I lost count after the fifth orgasm. During my last, I was a limp marionette, articulated only by the thrust of his hips and the brutal efficiency of his hands.

We've been in a state of frenzied euphoria with an insatiability for cupcakes and fucking. It dawns on me that we're doing something similar to the ancient followers of Dionysus—worshiping the god of overindulgence, through a state I can only describe as divine madness. *I wonder if this is part of the magic.*

Gage could keep going; he's still strong, still erect, and still smiling. But me? I am fully spent and seriously can't go another round.

Will the rest of my life be like this? Surely not. The other women in my family find time to do things other than fuck.

His breath is slow, deep, and content. He's pure muscle, smirking at me slightly smug, and incapable of hiding his pleasure.

But suddenly Gage shifts, and the arm he's got looped over my waist tightens, pinning me with a force I would call "protective."

"Alice," he whispers, tentatively, like he's not sure if talking is allowed.

"Hmm?"

"Are you going to throw me away?"

I twist around until I can see his face. He's already staring at me, eyes too blue to be real.

I prop myself up on an elbow. "No. Never."

He stares at me for a long, stunned second. "Okay. Good."

I flop back onto the pillow and stare at the ceiling. *Is this what he's been worried about?*

Gage is quiet for a while, but I can feel him thinking, cataloguing a thousand possible things to say next, then picks the one he thinks I want most. "Alice?"

"Yeah?"

"If I am staying…will I need a job?"

I can't help it—I lose it, laughing until my stomach hurts. "Oh, baby. You're the only person here less qualified to function in late-stage capitalism than I am."

He waits for the joke to end, then says, "But how will I help pay for things?"

"You don't have to," I say. "I just want you. Seriously. That's enough."

He processes this, and for a second, I see the wheels turning. "Okay," he says, then, "I want to help anyway. I can clean. Or cook."

"I'm not going to lie. I definitely need help with both those things," I say.

He nods, very solemn. "That is immediately apparent to anyone who sees your apartment or eats your burnt toast."

"Hey! You said you liked my toast."

"I did. I do. But then I made some myself and realized that there is better toast."

I laugh, loud. "I thought I couldn't do any wrong. I thought I was the thing everything is measured against."

He smiles and chuckles. "In this instance, you are not the maximum value. You are…the origin. There can be better or worse, positive or negative, relative to your toast."

Our giggles lapse into silence, and I study the curve of his jaw. He drums a pattern on my hip, and I think it's funny he's one of the few objects I didn't suspect would have trouble being still.

After a while, I say, "There's something I need to give you."

I reach for my phone, tilt it so he can see, unlock it, and scroll for a second.

I tap to my contacts and point at a picture of a middle-aged man, who I now realize is way too handsome to have not been magically conjured. "That's my dad."

He frowns, confused. "Your father?"

"Yeah," I say. "If you click here, you can call him. Or you can send him a text here."

"Why would I do that?"

"Well, I thought you might want to talk to him. He could help you with all your 'I used to be a ruler, now I'm a dude' questions."

He blinks, then blinks again, and I realize he's tearing up. Not in the sad way—just overwhelmed, maybe, or grateful.

"He can help you," I say, softer now. "And he can introduce you to the rest of the family. A lot of them are in the same boat."

Gage looks up, visibly lost. "What boat?"

I smother a laugh. "It's an expression. It means they're like you. They used to be objects, and now they're..." I make a sweeping gesture, "people, too."

He frowns, as if picturing an actual boat. "Is it a large boat?"

"I mean, I guess?" I try not to grin. "It's a metaphor. It just means there's a community for you. You're not alone in this, okay?"

He nods, the lines in his face going soft. "I would like to meet them."

I reach out and touch his hand. "Then you will."

He's quiet again, in that way I now know means he's going to ask me something soon. "Alice?"

"Yeah?"

He sighs, a little tragic. "There's a Sharpie in the junk drawer that's drying out." His face goes dark. "Please don't throw it away."

"A Sharpie?"

"Yeah. I recall being next to it when I lived in the junk drawer. It… is a comforting memory."

"Was the Sharpie, like, your friend or something?"

"'Friend' is not the correct term. But…I have a friendly fondness for it, yes."

I look at him, trying to convey the seriousness I know this moment requires, even though I have never once given a second thought about throwing away a dried-out Sharpie before. "Okay, yeah, I promise. I won't."

He's silent again, and I wait for the question I suspect is coming. "Would you consider…maybe giving it life?"

I choke on air. "Wait. Are you asking me to…fuck your friend?"

Gage doesn't hesitate. "The term 'friend' is still incorrect, but the idea is the same, so, yes."

I blink, considering what the personality of a Sharpie would be: probably sharp of wit and likes drawing dicks on everything.

I ask, "Like fuck it just to give it life or…?" I don't finish the question, unable to voice what I think he may be asking.

"I really want it to try cake. Also, I would appreciate its assistance in pleasing you sexually."

I stare at him in disbelief. I can't tell if I'm horrified or deeply, deeply intrigued. I laugh at the absurdity of it. It's so unbelievable that I have to consider it. "Just the Sharpie, or are there any nightstand objects you'd like me to give life? I could turn the vibrator into a human right now."

He looks horrified. "Absolutely not the vibrator."

I laugh. "Do you have beef with my vibrator?"

"Yes, it is a dick—literally and derogatorily."

I laugh a belly laugh, surprised I have the energy for it.

Then I look at him, really look: the wild hair, the stupidly perfect jaw, the hopeful, dorky expression. I could say no. I probably should say no.

But I don't.

Instead, I say, "I might need to change my stance on you getting a job. I can't keep up with the cupcake budget if we bring more objects to life."

Gage beams, incandescent. "I'd like that. I wanted a job anyway. I'm hoping there is a job I can use this with." He pulls the measuring tape out of somewhere as if he had it permanently attached to even his naked hip. He extends it, then snaps it back theatrically.

I laugh and kiss him hard, because what else can you do when your ruler boyfriend is asking you to fuck a Sharpie?

* * *

Want to know what happens when Alice grants Gage's "friend" life? Read *Marc: A Sentient Permanent Marker Romance.*

A NOTE FROM THE AUTHOR

Thank you so much for taking the time to read *Gage: A Sentient Ruler Romance.*

The idea for this book stemmed from a conversation I had with some author friends on Discord. I "pitched" the following idea:

> Midas's great, great, great granddaughter has a cursed pussy. But instead of everything that touches it turning to gold, it turns into an annoying guy she now has to be second-mommy to.
>
> Then mom will call and nag, "That's what you get for shoving a ruler up your pussy, sweety. You know how our curse works. Now you have a man-baby who is really particular about rules and numbers following you around."

Anyway, I have ADHD and tend to run with things 😁

Please leave a review on Amazon and Goodreads.

If you'd like to keep up with my work, follow me on social media and subscribe to my newsletter:

https://www.instagram.com/imogenknowed

https://www.imogenknowed.com/newsletter

SPECIAL THANKS

I want to thank my husband for his unwavering support while I wrote this book. Without his support, I could not have hyper-focused on it, writing literally every moment of the day that I wasn't working or sleeping.

To my husband:

Thank you for enthusiastically discussing characters and plot with me. Thank you for being okay with the fact that my mind was lost to another world for a while. Thank you for always putting food in front of me when I get so lost in something and forget my own body has needs. Thank you for always being there to help me recover whenever my mind and body explode from the world being too loud, too distracting, and too scratchy. I love you.

ABOUT THE AUTHOR

Imogen Knowed is a queer, AuDHD girly who hyperfocuses on creating fake people in her head. Instead of letting them stay in there, she writes them down for others to meet. She spends her days programming video games and her nights reading and writing smut. When she's not writing smut or making video games, she's hanging out with her family and pets (aka her "pack").

* * *

You can follow her on social media:

https://www.instagram.com/imogenknowed

https://www.threads.com/@imogenknowed

www.ingramcontent.com/pod-product-compliance
Lightning Source LLC
LaVergne TN
LVHW010627100826
845148LV00014B/3143

* 9 7 9 8 9 8 7 4 8 2 5 7 5 *